"I SHOULD NEVER HAVE MARRIED YOU FOR THE SAKE OF ADOPTING A CHILD!"

Noah met her glare, and the laughter died in his eyes. "Don't start that now, Maggie. I'll get you what you want, and nobody else can promise you that. If you want to keep this strictly business, then we will. But you've already agreed to our plan."

"It's a ridiculous plan," she answered angrily.

She felt the grip of his hand on her shoulder. "Let's stop playing games. It's too late now."

"Okay, I'll stop. Do what you have to do," she said with resignation.

"That's my girl." He took her chin between his thumb and forefinger and lifted her face. "Let's get on with it."

CANDLELIGHT ECSTASY ROMANCES®

SO MUCH TO GIVE

Sheila Paulos

A CANDLELIGHT ECSTASY ROMANCE®

Published by
Dell Publishing Co., Inc.
1 Dag Hammarskjold Plaza
New York, New York 10017

Dell ® TM 681510, Dell Publishing Co., Inc.

Candlelight Ecstasy Romance®, 1,203,540, is a registered
trademark of Dell Publishing Co., Inc., New York, New York.

ISBN: 0-440-18190-9

Printed in the United States of America

First printing—October 1985

For John, Leah, and Daniel, of course;
my aunt Rose, my mother-in-law, Helen;
my dear friends Mimi, Ellen, Robert, and
Judy; and last but not least, for Helen K.,
without whose unflagging encouragement
and inspiration I would still be making
soggy zucchini bread and wondering,
What am I going to do with my life?

To Our Readers:

We have been delighted with your enthusiastic response to Candlelight Ecstasy Romances®, and we thank you for the interest you have shown in this exciting series.

In the upcoming months we will continue to present the distinctive sensuous love stories you have come to expect only from Ecstasy. We look forward to bringing you many more books from your favorite authors and also the very finest work from new authors of contemporary romantic fiction.

As always, we are striving to present the unique, absorbing love stories that you enjoy most—books that are more than ordinary romance. Your suggestions and comments are always welcome. Please write to us at the address below.

Sincerely,

The Editors
Candlelight Romances
1 Dag Hammarskjold Plaza
New York, New York 10017

CHAPTER ONE

FOREIGN ADOPTION AGENCY ACCUSED OF SELLING BABIES! SHUT DOWN BY GOVERNMENT! The headlines that had screamed out at her from the morning newspaper reverberated in her mind, sending her into a tailspin of worry. During breakfast she had dropped a jar of apricot preserves, almost choked on her jellyless toast, and brewed her coffee to the consistency of mud. The rest of the day had been no better.

Maggie Clay, thirty-one, never married, and with no prospects in sight, ached to be a mother. Though she had thought about it, she did not, as a single woman, want to become pregnant herself. For one thing, she couldn't afford to give up her job in the advertising department of the *Minneapolis Sentinel*. For another, she didn't want to wind up in a position where she would be forever explaining herself to the rest of the world.

Maggie Clay wanted to adopt a child, and just about the only avenues open to her as an unmarried person were foreign adoption agencies. Unhappily there were only a few of these, and they were subject to the vagaries of foreign politics or public opinion. The agency she had been working with was based in India. Its reputation was solid, and she had been promised an infant daughter within the next six months. And now this! Even without knowing all the details Maggie suspected that the charges of baby-selling were trumped up, either by misguided nationalist politicians or by a muckraking reporter looking for a scoop.

She thought of the silly headline on the tabloid she had seen at the supermarket the day before—SCIENTISTS REVEAL WHY PEOPLE FEAR MURDER—and hoped the adoption story was just as empty of substance. She knew the agency's fees were not exorbitant. Selling babies indeed, she scoffed. The adoption support group she belonged to met in the union hall just north of the University of Minnesota campus that evening. If anyone knew the real story, they would.

Someone was speaking as she entered the small auditorium that night. A blowsy woman with carrot-colored hair whom she had heard speak on several previous occasions was standing behind the podium. What was she saying? Maggie could hardly make out the words. "Where there's a will, there's a way."

"Terrific." Maggie smiled to herself. For pearls of wisdom like that she shouldn't have bothered straining her ears. Anyway, that was easy enough for the redhead to say. She had a husband. For a married couple with several thousand dollars in legal fees and no great preference as to hair color or nationality, what she said was probably true. But Maggie was single, the only single person in the room. She raised her hand. Recognized by the chair, Maggie stood up.

"Does anyone have any information on the Child Faith Agency and the story about it in the *Sentinel* today? I was hoping to get a baby with them soon. What do I do now?" Maggie heard the slight quaver in her voice and didn't like it. Her eyes swept the room. Most of the mid-thirtyish faces were familiar to

10

her, hopeful faces that mirrored longing and frustration.

The redhead looked at her sympathetically. "We don't have information yet, but from experience I can tell you that no matter how baseless the charge, it will be a long time before any babies are released through that agency." The woman continued, but her voice became a drone as Maggie's spirits sank. Maggie thought of eating her toast and jelly alone in the morning.

From somewhere in the back of the auditorium she heard the large wooden doors open and shut as people entered and left. When the red-haired woman had stopped, Maggie asked almost plaintively, "But what can I do now?"

"We do have a list of attorneys who handle private placements abroad."

Maggie instinctively shook her head. The thought of lawyers making a profit from this sort of thing turned her stomach. Anyway, she didn't have very much money in her savings account. What she had would cover charges for adopting through a nonprofit agency and the extra expenses incurred by a baby for at least the first year. An attorney's fee would just about wipe her out.

"Then I'm afraid you'll have to go through the state," the woman said. "I don't know of another private agency that will work with single people."

"That can take years," Maggie said, her voice breaking. The redhead looked embarrassed and didn't answer. "Okay, thank you."

Sinking to her seat, it took Maggie a few moments to become aware of the earthy after-shave emanating from the previously vacant seat next to her.

"Hi, there." Maggie found herself looking at Noah Jamison, the controversial, pugnacious columnist of

11

the *Minneapolis Sentinel.* Although she had passed him several times in the *Sentinel* building, she had never met him. She'd never wanted to meet him, either. There was something about him that frightened her. It wasn't that his looks were bad, for he was undoubtedly handsome if you liked teddy bears. Maybe it was just that they were such different physical types. She was blond and petite with classically chiseled features. He was burly with shaggy dark hair and big chocolate eyes. He was the type of guy who made women want to hug him. With his lopsided grin that could usually lull even the most unsuspecting, he could be overwhelmingly charming. But Maggie saw a sharpness and a shrewdness underneath that had always made her wary of him. Whenever she saw him at work, she hurried her steps and studiously avoided meeting his eyes.

"Hi," she answered, letting her gaze fall briefly on him before turning her attention back to the podium. She had difficulty concentrating on the next speaker, however, and she suspected that the innocuous nature of the talk was but a small part of the reason. With a start she realized that Noah Jamison was in exactly the same position as she was. He had written a column about a month before dealing with the sad situation of single men who wanted to adopt. Suspected of all sorts of nasty things, they had an even harder time of it than single women. In his column he cited primate research that showed that male rhesus monkeys could quite easily adopt orphaned infant monkeys. Writing satirically Noah had wondered if neglecting to shave, growing his arms longer, and eating bananas by the bunch would increase his chances of getting a baby.

"What's your name?" Noah asked.

"Maggie Clay."

"Pleased and honored. I'm Noah Jamison."

Maggie looked straight at him. "I knew that."

Noah had the grace to flush. "I was standing in the back of the room before," he whispered. "I heard. I'm sorry."

Maggie nodded.

"That's rotten luck," he continued. "I was looking at that agency myself. Don't let it get you down, though. We'll work it out."

Maggie turned to look at him sharply. "We'll?"

"Where there's a we'll there's a way," he punned.

Maggie groaned. Noah Jamison had risen to prominence at the paper partly because his slant was different from that of the liberal paper he worked for. His hard-hitting punch was lightened with an unflagging optimism and humor. He was not a scold or a curmudgeon but more of a puckish satirist with a refreshingly clear way of viewing the world. Unfortunately she wasn't feeling very optimistic now, and she didn't want to be cajoled into looking at the bright side.

Noah turned in his seat to look straight into her eyes. She could tell that he was holding in a chuckle. "Why haven't we met before? You could be my best audience. Like, where have you been all my life?" His voice took on a mock hippie drawl.

"In the *Sentinel*'s advertising department. I've seen you plenty of times. You just never noticed me."

"Are you kidding?" He raised an eyebrow. "How could any man who calls himself a man not notice you? I noticed you every time we passed . . . but you weren't noticing me! I was shy."

"You, shy!" Maggie laughed to herself as she thought of his reputation. "You've got the biggest mouth in the Twin Cities."

"Only when I'm writing."

13

"You don't seem very shy right now." Maggie looked at him doubtfully.

"My toes are curled up in my shoes."

From the blank expression on his face Maggie couldn't tell whether or not he was serious. "I think you're putting me on," she said finally.

"Why would I do that?"

"You tell me."

"Come on," he said, grinning. "We're not going to get anything out of this meeting tonight. Let's go adopt a burger at McDonald's."

Maggie hesitated. Oh, what the heck, she decided. She hadn't eaten dinner, and she could use someone with whom to commiserate. She hadn't told any of her friends or family about her plan to adopt a baby. They'd tell her to buy a dog instead, or to find a husband. Then she'd have to say that dogs and husbands were nice, but she wanted a baby. No, thanks. She had decided to defer those conversations.

"Well?" Noah said impatiently, launching into a parody of the line about the lack of healthy infant babies prospective adoptive parents were given by all the agencies. "You realize there's only a limited number of burgers and long lines of people who want them, and if you want one that's hot and on a fresh bun, you'd better make up your mind soon!"

Maggie laughed. "You do have a way of making the most wretched situations funny."

"Tolerable, not funny," he said more seriously.

He was looking at her intently, brows lowered, eyes narrowed in a way that made goose bumps rise on her arms. She stood up, grabbing her purse and coat, and led the way up the aisle and out of the meeting. He was right behind her. She could have sworn that she felt his breath on the back of her neck, but then she decided that it was her imagination.

What nonsense! she thought, berating herself. He had only asked her to go out for a hamburger!

With a courtly flair that she wouldn't have expected from this rather rough-and-tumble columnist, he took her elbow to guide her across the street to his car.

"What about my car?" she asked. "Let's each drive and meet there."

"How about I drive us there and then I'll drive you back here?"

"Oh. Okay, I guess." Maggie stepped into his car, a sporty, mud-streaked import that had seen better years. As the seat of her cotton pants hit the seat of his car, she realized that there was something between her and the upholstery—a pair of dirty sneakers. Half rising, she reached under her and held them up by the gray shoelaces. "Nice."

"Just throw those in the back," Noah said unconcernedly.

As she did, her foot knocked against an old soda can, causing the few remaining drops of grape pop to spill out across her ankle. She looked down at the stain spreading across her shoe.

"There's a box of tissues around there somewhere." Noah's tone was helpful.

Maggie reached down and came up with a blackened peach pit and a tissue box that looked as if it had been rained upon. "I see the cleaning lady forgot to come this week."

Noah chuckled. "It's not that bad. Inoculations are not required before riding in this vehicle."

Maggie shook her head. "If your car is like this, I'd hate to see your house."

Glancing at her, Noah shifted gears. The car started with a jerk. "So, you want to adopt."

"That's right." Chewing on her bottom lip, Maggie looked out the window on the passenger side.

Minneapolis at night, she mused, was even lovelier than by day. Starlight in the sky and streetlights along the wide boulevards reflected off the mirror-smooth surfaces of the lakes. She counted three small lakes they had passed, just on this short journey. The well-kept parks that were used as road dividers lent the town a deceptively rural, almost innocent, ambience.

She stole a glance at Noah. In his navy-blue turtleneck sweater, his gray herringbone jacket, and his faded jeans he looked more like a thirty-five-year-old college professor who dressed young for his age than a tough, wisecracking newspaperman. Like his city, he, too, looked deceptively innocent. In profile, though, he traded his teddy-bear look for one of stalwart virility. He had a slightly long nose with a small bump in the middle where it must have been broken, thick eyebrows, jet-black lashes curled over piercing eyes, a strong jawline, and an olive complexion that could use two shaves a day. Her eyes lit on the hand that rested lightly on the steering wheel. His muscular arms ended in sensitive-looking hands with long, tapering fingers. She would expect squarer, stubbier-looking hands from a man of such apparent physical and psychological command.

Oblivious of the thoughts running through Maggie's mind, Noah asked conversationally, "Did you read my column?"

Instinctively aware of which one he meant, Maggie nodded. "Who didn't? It was very poignant."

"So why didn't you come and tell me that we had something in common?" Noah's voice was perplexed.

"I didn't see any reason to do that. It wouldn't have

helped either one of us, and common problems are no basis for a friendship." The words tumbled out of her mouth almost as if they hadn't originated in her brain. She took a deep breath. "I'd rather talk about the column you did on Italian food, the one where you said you never met a pasta you didn't like."

"Are you hinting that I take you to an Italian restaurant?"

"No, but that was one of the few columns you ever wrote that I totally agreed with. Anyway, I'm just subtly letting you know that there are some things I'd rather not talk about."

He raised his eyebrows, then winked. "Thanks for being subtle. So! Are you having cheese on your burger?"

Embarrassed, Maggie allowed a note of sarcasm to edge into her voice. "You can get a little more personal than that."

"Do you use roll-on or spray deodorant?" Noah asked, his face dead-pan.

Laughing, Maggie shook her head.

"What?" Noah pursued with mock amazement. "No deodorant? Anyway, you do smell like a rose, you know. And me, I always come out smelling like a rose, no matter what the situation."

"I'll remember that," Maggie said lightly.

"Yes, do," he responded jauntily. Noah, it seemed, never let a metaphor drop. "Speaking of roses, the scent of french fries is beginning to permeate the atmosphere. We must be closing in on the burger orphanage." Pulling into the lot, he parked the car and reached over Maggie's lap to open her door. "I hope your papers are in order."

"Yes, here they are," Maggie announced, playing along and hoping she would make it clear that she was not interested in any other games with Noah.

17

She pulled some single dollar bills out of her purse and held them out to him.

Pushing her hand away, Noah said a bit more harshly than Maggie deemed necessary considering their relationship, "I'll take care of the green papers." The ensuing silence as they walked into the fast-food restaurant was uncomfortable.

Seated in the bright plastic booth across from Noah, Maggie took a self-consciously dainty bite out of her hamburger. It had been years, she realized, since she had given a thought to how she looked as she bit into a bun. But the way Noah was staring at her, as if he were making some sort of feature-by-feature assessment for auction, was making her nervous.

"How old are you, Maggie?"

Should she lie? Maggie briefly considered saying she was twenty-five. With her smooth peaches-and-cream complexion, firm skin, small stature, and gay laugh, she knew she could get away with it. But there was no reason to lie, she told herself, pushing vanity aside. "Thirty-one," she answered with only the slightest falter in her voice.

Noah gave a curt nod as if making a notation on a mental checklist.

"You ever been arrested?"

Almost choking, Maggie shook her head. This was absurd, she thought, but then decided to be a good sport about it. She laughed. "But I am a spy for a foreign country." She took a long sip of her Coke. "I'd say you're quite a conversationalist. Why are you asking me these questions?"

"I want to know about you."

"What do you want to know?"

"Everything." He said it seriously.

18

Maggie laughed. "Well, when I'm not spying, I'm a Democrat. Chuckles are my favorite candy—I save the black one for last—and I'm a compulsive neatnik when it comes to cars. Houses are a different story. What about you?"

Noah grinned. "Well, I'm more or less a Republican. I'm dedicated to tracking down beautiful blond spies, especially if they wear gray fedoras slouched over one eye and belted trench coats, a combination, which for your edification, I can't resist. I hate Chuckles with the possible exception of the red one, and I can't drive unless I'm sitting in pretzel crumbs. I like my house antiseptic, though."

Maggie gaily popped a french fry into her mouth. "So much for compatibility. I wouldn't, by the way, be caught dead in a trench coat or a fedora."

"I've got one more question for you, Maggie."

"Yes?" Maggie's manner was exaggeratedly demure. Since deciding to play along, she was actually enjoying this little encounter. "What's your question?"

"Oh, nothing much. I'm free next Friday, and that would give you time to get your affairs in order. So, I was just wondering if you'd marry me then?"

CHAPTER TWO

Maggie chewed on the tip of her pencil's eraser. She hadn't been doing much selling for the newspaper the last couple of days. Her desultory, preoccupied manner communicated itself to prospective advertisers. The other night's business proposal had caught her off-guard. It had taken Noah the rest of the evening to convince her that he was serious. It was the only way, he claimed, that they could each be successful in their quest for a child. Once the waiting periods were over, they could get a divorce and go their separate ways, each with a child of their own. The marriage would be in name only.

Very neat and tied with a bow. Except that Maggie had never liked surprise presents. She nodded absently as the courier brought in the morning edition. After glancing at the front-page news, Maggie read the people section and the local columnists before checking on the ads she was responsible for. Even when not enthusiastic about her job, she was conscientious.

In the adjoining cubicle she heard Jennifer Martin, who worked in personals, giggling about something. Since she giggled more or less constantly, Maggie didn't pay much attention to Jennifer until she came over and sat down in front of her desk. "Listen, Maggie, you've got to read this ad I just received."

"Shoot, Jen." Maggie tried successfully to disguise her daydreaming. Jen was a sweet girl of eighteen, full of enthusiasm and bounce.

"I just received it a few minutes ago. I hope I got it right." Jennifer was breathless from it all. "Here goes: 'Wanted: Wife for purposes of adopting baby. Thirty-one years old, petite blond, no experience required. Background in espionage or advertising helpful. Salary negligible, rewards incalculable, terms of agreement negotiable. Write LULLABYE, P.O. Box 4532, Minneapolis, Minnesota 55430. All responses held in strictest confidence.' "

Maggie blinked and spilled a few drops of coffee on her lap. She read the ad again. She wanted to laugh but couldn't. "Did you get a phone number for this?"

Jennifer put her hand over her mouth. "Oh, my gosh. I forgot. Can we still run it without a phone number? Who will we bill? What if it's a hoax? Oh, this is such a high-pressure job!"

"Take it easy, Jennifer. It's okay. Don't worry. We can send the bill to the P.O. box he gave you." The girl seemed genuinely upset at not having followed strict protocol. Maggie remembered when she began at the paper and worked in the want-ads department. She was told to be careful about the word count of her classifieds. She must have spent half her time rewriting the ads to make them shorter for her customers. "It's all right, Jen."

Still slightly chastened at her minor oversight, Jennifer returned to her little cubicle. Maggie sat wondering about the ad. She suddenly feared that Noah might make this whole adoption business with her a public affair in his next column. She feared that he might be capable of such a thing. Whatever slight interest she had in the scheme should have evaporated completely at the thought.

Still, the proposition intrigued her, and she found herself thinking about it almost all the time. It was a seductively easy way to get what she so desperately wanted without the complications of unwed motherhood. If he could be trusted to really keep things confidential, Noah seemed capable—capable and less likely to become entangled in adoption red tape and double talk than she would be. He had a reputation for end-runs around regulations and rules at the newspaper. He would know how to get things done quickly and efficiently. The borderline nature of his idea stimulated her too. Noah's very name and the images of starting over on the ark that it conjured up seduced her into action.

She decided to grab the bull whose name was Noah by the horns and at least explore this zany proposal a little further. Unwilling to use her office phone for fear of being overheard, she grabbed a handful of change from her purse and went out to use the pay phone in the building's lobby to call him at home.

"Noah Jamison," he barked into the phone.

Her heart was racing. "This is Maggie."

"And this is a pleasant surprise." His voice, though soft, held a hint of laughter. "What can I do for you, Maggie?"

"The ad . . ." she began.

"Are you my first respondent?" he cut in amusedly.

She bit her lower lip and frowned. "I was simply calling to discuss the ad with you. I'm not sure how appropriate it is, given your stated intentions."

"The word *appropriate* is not in my vocabulary. I don't know what it means. I know what want and desire and hunger mean, though. You know, Maggie, I just woke up and I'm starving. Care to join me for some breakfast?"

22

"I'm at work, and I already ate," she answered curtly.

"Meet me at 824 Dallas Road in Brooklyn Park." The address was a middle-class suburb of Minneapolis. "I have a present to give you."

"No, thanks."

"Well, then, I have something to show you."

Maggie laughed. "You don't give up, do you?"

"Meet me there in an hour. You won't regret it." The click of the phone resounded in her ear. Maggie looked at the silent receiver and wrinkled her nose. Noah Jamison was one of the most presumptuous men she had ever met, and she'd come across quite a few in her time. Unfortunately he was also one of the most attractive.

On his end Noah Jamison sat looking at his silent phone as well. A big, self-satisfied grin played across his face. It was going well, he mused. She would bite. He leaned back in his leather chair, his hands clasped behind his head, his legs stretched out in front of him. He surveyed versions of his half-written column spread out around his cluttered desk and smiled.

Closing his eyes, he pictured Maggie. Though not exactly petite, she was almost doll-like in appearance and had such a childlike innocence about her that it was hard for him to believe that she was all of thirty-one years old. But he knew she was telling the truth. He had checked with personnel at the paper. After that, he had gotten a detective friend of his to do a more thorough check on her background.

He gave a small laugh. Maggie Clay didn't have the dark, exotic looks of the women who usually attracted him, but she had a kind of quiet, understated magnetism about her that bowled him over like a semi-trailer. He couldn't get her out of his mind. When he thought of her, he could almost feel his chest expand. She made him feel protective and strong, a little like King Kong. Well, at least the thought of her made him feel that way. The reality he'd find out about soon enough.

Maggie looked at her new digital watch and noted that it was showing the date. She pressed one of the little buttons along the edge of the watch case. Nothing happened. With a sigh, she looked at the wall clock in the lobby. It said 9:20. Her hair and clothes, though acceptable for a humdrum day at the office, were not suitable for a meeting with her potential spouse and father of her children. What was she getting herself into? She steeled herself and willed her doubts to disappear.

"Jennifer, if anyone calls for me, tell them I'm out seeing an important client."

"Oh, Miss Clay, advertising seems so exciting. I hope you get the account."

"I'll get it if I want it." Maggie looked troubled. "I just don't know if I want it."

Her mouth agape, Jennifer stared at her boss uncomprehendingly.

"I'm leaving instructions on my desk, Jen. Think you can handle the office for a while?"

"Uh, no."

"Sure you can. Just take it easy." Maggie smiled sympathetically at the nervous girl and thought ruefully that it would be nice if she could follow her own advice about taking it easy. Her stomach was doing double time, and her head was beginning to pound. "Nervous tension," she said, groaning aloud, "thy name is woman."

Maggie headed home for a quick change of clothes and a shower. Suddenly hypercritical of her appearance, she decided that her hair looked as though she had plugged herself into an electrical outlet that

24

morning. The skirt she was wearing was spotted from the coffee she had spilled on it earlier, and her new panty hose had gotten into the spirit of things by developing two symmetrical runs.

Maggie breathed a sigh of relief when she pulled in front of her apartment building. She sat behind the wheel for a few seconds, her eyes closed. The thought of a hot stream of water pounding between her shoulder blades propelled her into action and up the four flights of stairs to her "picturesque" loft in a converted warehouse. In a city renowned for its lakes and parks and split-level homes, the converted warehouse on the edge of the city's downtown area was a sort of odd place to call home, but that was part of its appeal for Maggie.

The loft had, in fact, turned out to be less than Maggie's dream house. Oh, it was true that there was a skylight. But it was also true that there was a crack in it, and when it snowed that first November, a week after she had moved in, Maggie could have built a snowman in her living room. Now it was patched with some transparent plastic sheeting and glue. Then there were the cats. For some reason a whole collection of cats would gather in the narrow street underneath her sleeping alcove every night and serenade her with howls and wails. It was eerie, and it had taken some getting used to. The faucet in the kitchen sink leaked constantly, the rust stain in the basin was getting darker by the day, and the landlord turned a deaf ear to all of Maggie's importunings.

But Maggie loved the romance—if not the reality —of living in a loft. It was hers, and it had wonderful exposed beams. And where else could she see the stars at night when she lay in her bed? It had so much more character than the apartments she had lived in before. So there were inconveniences! So walking up four flights when you were balancing three grocery bags was not her idea of aerobic exercise! Her loft had soul, and soul was a rare commodity these days. She wished she didn't have to be defensive about it. She wasn't telling her mother or her friends or colleagues to move in with her or pay the rent! Live and let live. That was her motto.

All these thoughts passed through Maggie's mind as she climbed the stairs, threw her coat on a chair, and dropped her clothes on her bed, strewn with adoption literature. She hurried to the shower, pausing only to lay out a new outfit on her bed, a deep blue short-sleeved knit sweater that was the exact shade of her eyes and a pair of cream-colored cords. Opening a fresh bar of soap, she turned on the shower.

"Oh, no!" she protested, groaning aloud. The hot water was out again. Great timing! Gritting her teeth, she turned on the cold water and lathered up. She decided that her hair would have to do as it was. Frizz and let frizz, she thought to herself with a chuckle. That would be her second motto.

As she drove out to the address in Brooklyn Park Maggie wondered why in heaven's name she was going there. When she came up with no good reason, she concentrated instead on appreciating the beauty of the drive. Minneapolis, her adopted city, was one of the most pleasant cities in the country. Maggie had known that the day she arrived there from the small town across the border in northern Wisconsin where she had grown up. Her hometown boasted much natural beauty but little by way of diversion. That was the reason every other person there, it seemed to her, had a drinking problem. Minneapolis, by contrast, was brimming with interesting shops, restaurants, shows, and museums. In addition to all the lakes and parks within its limits, it was clean and had very little crime. Maggie's parents saw it that way too. After they had visited their daughter a few times it was not too difficult to convince them to move there. They, in turn, convinced much of the rest of the family to move there. The city was a well-kept secret, gaining its popularity by word of mouth, and its people aimed to keep it that way. Among themselves they often called it Minneapple, the little Big Apple of the Midwest.

Maggie left her car windows open. The spring breeze felt good on her face and couldn't make her hair any worse. Thinking about Noah's ad, she felt herself becoming angry. He must really think her a little flaky to go along with his harebrained plan. Obviously one flake was as good as the next to him. If she wouldn't fall for the scheme, he would advertise for someone else. And to think that she was almost really considering it! So why, if she were feeling this way, had she taken the morning off work to come out to Brooklyn Park? The obvious answer was that she was still flirting with the idea.

Wandering around the neat suburban streets, Maggie had some difficulty finding the address on Dallas Road. When she finally did, the first thing that caught her eye was the redwood deck on the side of the house and the beautiful evergreens in the front. It was an attractive house but hardly the type of place she would have pictured Noah Jamison in. This was a house for a family with a dog and a station wagon.

As if it had read her thoughts, a barking Irish setter came out to greet her as she pulled into the driveway. Noah was not far behind. Wearing a pair of baggy, plaid polyester slacks she never would have believed of him and a cardigan sweater, he looked like he belonged with the house. As if to drive the point home, he was steering an electric lawn mower with a large canvas bag to collect the grass in back.

"You've come at last. Let me welcome you to the future home of Baby X and Baby Y," he said in greeting.

"You look the part of a nice old dad," she answered dryly, "but you didn't have to dress for me. I'm not the social worker."

With a big roar of laughter Noah ripped off his sweater, unzipped his pants, and, hopping on one leg at a time, pulled them off. He revealed himself in the faded jeans and tight turtleneck she had grown accustomed to seeing in the halls of the *Sentinel* offices. With his change of clothes, the familiar cocky tilt of his head returned. "Here he is, ladies and gentlemen, Noah Jamison in all his splendor." He said it with a flourish as if he expected a round of applause.

Maggie just stared.

"Here he is, ladies and gentlemen—"

"I heard you the first time," Maggie cut in.

"Oh, then let me show you this humble abode and give you what you came for."

"What did I come for?"

"Your present, of course."

"Noah, I don't want your presents. I don't want anything from you."

His voice was patient, as if he were talking to a child. "Then why did you come?"

"To discuss the ad with you."

"Do you do all of your business in person?"

Caught, Maggie felt her face reddening. "Why did you call in that ridiculous ad?"

"Ridiculous?" Noah pretended he was brought up short. "I hadn't thought of it like that. Well, pull it then."

"Just like that? You want me to pull it?"

28

"Sure. It served its purpose already."

Maggie's stomach did flip-flops. She didn't have to ask what purpose. "You manipulated me."

"Yep. Is that so bad?"

"And you want to use me."

"In a manner of speaking, right again."

Caught at an impasse—the starkly spoken truth—they stared silently at each other. Noah's eyes held a dare. Maggie's eyes were guarded. She felt herself pulled in two directions. On the one hand, Noah presented a fairly simple solution to her dilemma. On the other, his scheme seemed, if not actually illegal, slightly immoral. Well, not exactly immoral, but bizarre. Yes, it was a bizarre plan. And the closest Maggie had ever come to "bizarre" was in renting her converted warehouse loft. For most of her life she had walked the straight and narrow. She had usually done what was expected of her and shunned the unexpected. No one could ever say that Maggie Clay's socks didn't match, she thought wryly.

Noah grinned diabolically and made his voice resonate in a timbre that Maggie guessed was supposed to sound like a vampire.

"Won't you come in now so that I can put my evil plan into action?" He gave a bloodcurdling chuckle, then smiled almost shyly, as if aware of how silly this swaggering act of his was.

Maggie shrugged. She was already here, so she may as well find out what this was all about.

The house was done in rented Danish-American furniture and motel-style pictures. The decor, if nothing to write home about, was inoffensive. It went well with plaid polyester. In the center of the living room was an enormous white box tied with a red ribbon.

29

Noah gestured toward the box. "Aren't you going to open it?"

"Do I have to?" Maggie giggled nervously.

"I'll bar the doors and hold you prisoner until you accede to my wishes." His eyes held a twinkle and something else Maggie couldn't quite divine.

Goose bumps rose on her arms, much to Maggie's embarrassment. She tugged at her sleeves and wished that she had worn a long-sleeved shirt rather than this off-season knit pullover. Raising her eyes to his, she saw that he was watching her intently and knew that he had read her thoughts.

She decided to be flip. "I'll bet it's a blender. Just what I need."

He smiled. "I'll get you a blender next time." His eyes shifted to the white box. "What are you waiting for?" Noah took a step toward her and then seemed to hesitate. He was an odd combination of bluster and tentativeness, Maggie thought.

"Maybe you should give me a grand tour of your house first."

Noah sighed impatiently, comfortably back in his bully role. "Come on, Maggie. It's a bi-level. You've seen one bi-level, you've seen them all."

Maggie was surprised. "That's no way to talk about your home."

The glance he shot her was quizzical. Didn't she understand? he wondered.

Not knowing quite what to do, Maggie laughed again. "Well, I might as well open it. It feels like Christmas. Such a big box."

"And it's square too."

Feeling the impatience in his sarcasm, Maggie knelt and untied the bow. Then she scraped away the tape holding the paper together so that it wouldn't rip and carefully folded the wrapping paper.

"I've never seen anything opened so carefully," Noah said, trying to mask his eagerness. "I'm of the school that believes in ripping wrapping."

"Score one more point for incompatibility," Maggie teased as she lifted the lid. Faced with a mountain of tissue paper, she laughed. "Whatever it is, it must be fragile." She folded the tissue paper in a slow, methodical way, purposely trying to rouse his impatience.

"It is fragile." Noah's voice was grave.

Gingerly, so as not to accidentally break the contents, Maggie emptied the box. At the very bottom nestled on a pad of jeweler's cotton lay a shiny key. She held it up. "What's this?"

"The key to my hopes and dreams . . . and to the front door." Again the flippant intonation revealed more feeling than was intended.

Maggie drew in a sharp breath. When she exhaled, she closed her eyes halfway and looked hesitantly at Noah. "Don't try to bamboozle me into anything."

"Why not? You're too stubborn to see the light by yourself. If you want P, and in order to get P you must do Q, then you do Q in order to get P. It's only elementary human logic."

"You mind your Ps and Qs and I'll mind mine. I'm not moving into your house and that's that!"

"This isn't my house. It's *our* house. You don't actually think I would live out in the suburbs with four bedrooms, swing set in the backyard, and finished basement, do you? I leased it for us."

"Did you lease the dog too?" she asked sarcastically as the big dog came lumbering in and proceeded to destroy the neat pile of tissue and wrapping paper.

"No. I'm dog-sitting for a friend. He looks good here, though. Maybe I should borrow him for a while." Noah smiled sardonically. "Tell me, what so-

31

cial worker that you know is going to give babies to someone who lives in a factory warehouse? I'm going to have to pull enough strings as it is without having to explain that."

"How do you know where I live?" she shot back.

"I did some checking. There's a lot I know about you besides your age and what color Chuckles you prefer."

Maggie blanched. "That's an invasion of privacy!"

"Probably. But it goes on all the time. Besides, it was rather a small invasion."

"You had no right to do that!" she insisted doggedly.

"I had every right in the world. I wouldn't put my future in just anyone's hands. If you hadn't passed my rather rigorous scrutiny, if I can so modestly claim, I would have let this whole idea drop. But you came out clean as a whistle, no problems at all."

"You're crazy, you know that?" she shouted. "And you've got a lot of nerve! Just who do you think you are?"

"Your husband-to-be, Maggie Clay."

Striding over to the window, Maggie folded her arms over her chest. Her heart was thudding, and the palms of her hands were moist—especially the one that was holding the now-slippery key. She put the key on the windowsill. When she spoke, the pitch of her voice was unnaturally high. "Maybe I should get you investigated too!"

"I've already had myself investigated. I came out smelling like a rose. I told you I always do. They must have missed a few youthful indiscretions." He grinned and continued triumphantly, "Then you agree that my plan is brilliant?"

"I didn't say that."

"But you'll go along with it," he persisted.

"I didn't say that, either."

He moved across the room with a stealth that was almost primitive. Before she could react, he had grasped her upper arm in a powerful grip and turned her around. Shrugging her shoulder, she tried unsuccessfully to shake him off. With his other hand he lifted her chin so that she was looking up into his eyes. Her consciousness was filled with the darkness and depth of those eyes, with the sensation of his hand on the tip of her chin. When she momentarily lowered her gaze, she was struck by the feathering of black hair that covered the backs of his hands. He slid sensitive fingers farther up, almost to the juncture of arm and body. She shivered. It seemed an erotic, almost indecent, assault.

"Maggie." His voice was still urgent, yet soft. It was the voice of lovemaking, not of deal-making. "This doesn't have to be an unpleasant experience, you know." She felt his warm breath on her face.

"Listen, Noah, if I'm going to go through with this, and it looks like I am because I want a child more than anything else in the world, it has to be strictly a business arrangement." She paused and then continued almost harshly. "Do you understand?"

Noah nodded. Her vehemence seemed to please him.

CHAPTER THREE

"I told her that my daughter was a career woman.
'It's a new age today,' I said. 'Women don't have to be
housewives anymore. They can choose their way.'"
Maggie's mother took a small sip of her tea, then set
the china cup carefully down on the wooden crate
that masqueraded unsuccessfully as a coffee table.
She pursed her meticulously outlined red lips, a sure
sign that she would fight her daughter's battles till
the end, no matter what her own personal opinion
might be. . . .

"What did Aunt Mae say to that, Mom?"

"Never mind."

"Come on. What did she say?"

"She said"—her mother leaned forward—"that if
you could get married, you would jump at the
chance. She said I was making excuses because you
were unlucky in love."

"Aunt Mae said that?" Maggie laughed, though she
felt a tightness in her chest.

"And then I told her it was better not to ever get
married than to do what her Sally had done and
marry a flabby shoe salesman who always looked at
your feet when he talked to you." Maggie's mother
was warming up to her subject. "I said it was better to
spend every evening in front of the television set
than to be like her precious Susie and go out with

34

forty-two-year-old men who still lived at home with their mothers and had a curfew and green teeth."

"Green teeth, no less," Maggie echoed, actually starting to enjoy the story. "Then what did she say?"

Maggie's mother snorted. "She said you should be so lucky!"

"I'll bet you got her then, Mom."

Her mother remained silent. She toyed with the gold-rimmed cup Maggie had picked up at a rummage sale expressly for her mother's visits.

"Well, Mom. The suspense is killing me. I'll bet you came up with a zinger."

Her mother shook her head. "Then she told me the news." She looked around the sofa as if she had dropped something. "Your cousin is expecting."

Maggie froze. "Sally?"

Her mother's voice was unnaturally high-pitched. "Your little cousin, Sally. Yes. Well, now. Where is my hat? I'd better get a move on—so many things to do."

"Little Sally and the shoe salesman? That's wonderful. At least the baby will be well heeled." She tried to hide her jealousy.

Her mother sniffed. "Jokes, jokes. Perhaps you should try to be a little more serious. Men don't like women who are too witty."

"Mother . . ." Maggie's voice held a warning.

"Don't you 'mother' me. Now, then, you said you were going to help me run one of the food booths at the church bazaar on Saturday."

Maggie sighed. Ever since she could remember her mother had been drafting her to work on one or another of her pet projects. "What time do you want me to come over?"

"Two o'clock, dear. Don't be late. You know how important this is. You'll see your cousins there, so you'll be able to congratulate Sally in person."

"Super."

Maggie's digital kitchen clock said nine A.M. It was hard to believe that her mother had already breezed in and out, having stopped in on her daughter before a hard day of shopping in town. Maggie was beginning to regret having used a vacation day to stay home. She felt as though she needed a vacation day from her vacation day, and she was only an hour into it! With her mother's departure Maggie collapsed into the nearest chair. Then she had a better idea. She took a package of chocolate cupcakes from a kitchen cabinet, retrieved a new magazine from the living room, and slipped into bed. Once in bed, however, she no longer felt like reading. Forget the magazine! she thought. Instead she flipped on her television set using the remote control device she had treated herself to last Christmas.

"We have an unusual show for you today, ladies and gentlemen."

The voice of the popular television talk-show host blasted her out of her lethargy. "We have three women here who have opted for single motherhood."

Maggie groaned. First her mother, now this. There must be a conspiracy against her. Despite her initial reaction, however, Maggie sat up a bit straighter. The women who smiled into the camera seemed to be smiling directly at Maggie. When they began to speak, Maggie was mesmerized. They were so self-assured, so confident, so determined. Maggie envied them.

Before deciding to adopt a baby, Maggie had toyed with the idea of having one of her own, out of wedlock. But there were so many reasons not to. There were financial reasons, practical reasons that had to do with her career. And there was the sheer difficulty

36

of the pregnancy with no one to lend a hand or to lay that hand on a swollen abdomen in order to feel the kicking of tiny feet. But more than that, Maggie knew in her heart of hearts that there was a larger reason.

It was a reason that had to do with character and strength. Oh, she was a good person and she was strong, but her strength went only so far. It went far enough to raise a baby and care for it and love it. But she didn't think she would be able to cope with society's prejudices against single women who bore children. She didn't think she could stand the snide glances and whispered comments. She wouldn't be able to answer the sanctimonious people who would say she was an unfit mother and an immoral person without losing her cool.

Maggie was hotheaded. She didn't handle people well. She was unlike that marvelous talk-show host who was now handling a caller.

"Why don't these ladies adopt a handicapped child or become foster parents to troubled children instead of bringing a child with no father into the world?" a tinny voiced and undoubtedly tight-lipped caller asked.

"Now that's a real interesting question, ma'am," the shuffling TV host answered. "You raise quite a point there." He ducked his head and smiled disarmingly. "But you know, a lot of people could ask that question of married couples too. Have you adopted a handicapped child? Are you a foster mother? Those are real worthwhile commitments for anyone."

"N-no. I have children of my own." The woman was momentarily on the defensive.

"Well, they're all our children, aren't they?" the host continued relentlessly.

Maggie sat bolt upright in bed. "Bravo," she said to

her four walls. "A man of reason." But how many people were out there whose sentiments echoed those of the caller? Lots, she would reckon. Raising a child was hard enough without always having to defend its right to exist. No, Maggie did not want, as a single woman, to have a biological child. She wouldn't be able to handle the flak. An adopted child would claim her heart just as well. She had no doubts about that.

Maggie looked unseeingly at the commercial on her set. There was something else too. By adopting a child she not only wouldn't have to grapple with some people's prejudices, but also she would earn some others' admiration. How self-sacrificing and loving they would think her to be. And it would all be true. Maggie grimaced. All right, she thought, maybe that wasn't the most important aspect, but it did matter to her. Maybe it shouldn't. Maybe what others thought of her should be neither here nor there. But she wasn't perfect. She didn't even come close. But she wasn't all that bad, either, she decided. If her motivations weren't crystal-clear and pure as the driven snow, so what? The undeniable truth was that the most important thing in the world to her was having a little baby to love.

The ringing of the phone caused her to start. It had been a whole week since she had installed a new store-bought telephone, but she was still not used to the shrill sound of its ring.

"Is this Mrs. Wonderful?" Noah's voice sang out.

"You've got the wrong number, mister. This is Mrs. Moron speaking."

Noah laughed. "The only conceivably moronic thing about you is that you don't recognize how wonderful you are."

"Oh? Tell me about it. Better yet, let me tell you something—"

"Don't tell me you're having second thoughts," Noah broke in.

"Second? I'm up to twentieth!"

"Maggie! I'm surprised at you."

"Don't act surprised. When was the last time you asked someone you hardly knew to marry you and she accepted?"

"I don't propose and tell," he answered fliply. "What's the problem?"

"The problem is"—she paused to gather her thoughts—"that I don't know you and I don't love you, and what am I doing even thinking of marrying you?" Her tone changed from impassioned to self-righteous. "Marriage is a sacred institution."

"Amen."

Her voice rose. "Is that all you have to say?"

"No."

The line was pregnant with silence and then was filled with static.

"What's wrong with your phone?" he shouted over the noise.

"It's new," she answered as if in explanation.

"I'm coming right over." He hung up the phone without a good-bye, almost as though he were in such a rush to talk to her in person that he could take no time for such amenities.

For a moment she stood still, the dead phone an odd-looking growth between her ear and her shoulder. Then her immobility gave way to a flurry of activity. She shook the crumbs off her sleeves and chest. Cupcake crumbs were not exactly elegant, especially when you were wearing them. She made her bed, shoved the magazine underneath it, and threw the cupcake wrappers in the trash. It was, after all, ten o'clock in the morning, and unmade beds, magazines, and cupcakes were not the sort of thing you wanted anyone to know about you, especially someone you were considering marrying, for however brief a spell.

Checking herself in the mirror, she was horrified. Her hair was sticking up in a cowlick, her mascara from the night before was smudged under her eyes, and a pimple was starting on the side of her mouth. How come every time she was about to see Noah she looked her absolute worst? Well, he couldn't be marrying her for her looks or her money!

Quickly dressing in tight blue jeans and a sexy silk blouse, she surveyed the finished product in the mirror. She smiled with satisfaction. The only thing was, she mused, she didn't look very maternal. Well, so what! He wasn't the social worker.

There was a brusque knock on the door. Flinging the door open, she smiled in greeting.

"Why didn't you ask who it was?" he grumbled without giving her a chance to say hello.

"I was expecting you."

"I could have been a hatchet murderer."

"Or worse yet, you could have been my future mother-in-law," she cracked.

"No mother-in-law jokes allowed," he said with just the barest hint of a grin. "Seriously, you should never open the door to strangers. You have a peephole you didn't look through and a chain lock you didn't use. You had better change those ways when you're living in my house."

Maggie gulped. "You want to run that by me again?"

Suddenly aware of what he had said, Noah stammered. "What . . . what I, uh, mean is that you might, uh, think about being a little more, uh, care-ful."

"In *whose* house?" she snapped.

"In our house," he answered promptly, an honest-to-goodness blush starting up his neck.

Maggie sucked in her cheeks. "If I go along with you, this is going to be a one-to-one, completely equal business partnership. I thought I'd made that clear."

"As clear as your complexion," he said with a twinkle.

Involuntarily her hand went to the pimple at the corner of her mouth. She glared at him. "That was mean."

Noah held out his hands to her. "I didn't even notice that silly little blemish. I meant to give you a compliment."

Ignoring his proffered hands, she turned her back to him. "Well, you blew it."

She flinched as his hands came to rest on her shoulders. "My dear, you're being too sensitive. You're acting"—he paused and twisted his mouth mockingly, an expression she did not see—"almost as if you had some real emotional stake in our . . . relationship."

Noah had scored a bull's-eye, and Maggie felt as if she were dangling from his deftly inserted arrow. Still, she instinctively denied his accusation. "Listen, this is a business deal where hopefully we'll both get what we want—a child for each of us—and nothing more. I'd appreciate it, therefore, if you kept your half-baked, erroneous speculations to yourself. Do you understand?"

"Not quite. Maybe a blackboard and chalk would help. You could diagram your sentences, draw a few illustrations, and then maybe give me some true-false or multiple-choice questions to test me."

"I don't think that's necessary. You're a bright boy."

"A boy, am I?" Noah laughed, but his tone was clipped and impatient. "Listen, as long as we're explaining things to each other, let me make something clear. I've gone through a lot of agony already, and I'm going to go through a lot more trouble and expense with this venture of ours, so I don't want a certain bright girl changing her mind about it every few days. Do you understand?"

Maggie was touched by his use of the word *agony*. Pleased that he was quite serious about his desire for a child, her mood softened. "No, I don't understand. I think I need a diagram or two." She brushed a stray cupcake crumb from her sleeve, offering him a gentle smile. "I'm keeping this apartment, though, even if I partially move into that house of yours."

"House of *ours*," Noah amended.

"Okay, house of ours. But I'm self-sufficient now, and I intend to remain so."

"What does that mean, Maggie?" Noah affected a wearily patient attitude.

"It means that I'm going to pay my own way and not live beyond my means. Besides keeping this apartment, I'll give you half the rent each month for the house, buy my own food, and pay all my other expenses."

"Can you afford to do all that?"

"I can't afford not to."

"Okay, let's plan for the wedding."

"What? Now?"

"Why wait? We should be married for a while before we apply for adoption. I've already found a doctor who'll write a letter testifying to my irreversible vasectomy."

"I didn't know you'd had a vasectomy."

"I didn't, but the doctor doesn't know that."

"Noah Jamison." Maggie looked at the cocky tilt to his head and smiled. "I don't think I approve of this dishonest stuff at all."

"Sure you do, but you like to pretend you don't."

Maggie felt her chest constrict. His carelessly flung out words stung. "I'm a moral person."

"I didn't say you weren't."

"Dishonesty isn't moral," she snapped.

Noah grabbed her forearm. "Listen, Maggie . . ."

She pulled away.

"Listen, Maggie," he started again, this time with an unmistakable sneer, "I never said you were dishonest or immoral, but what I am saying is that you're coy. I don't like coy women. When you agreed to this deal, you knew we weren't going to tell the adoption agency that this was a mere marriage of convenience to be terminated at the earliest possible opportunity. So don't lay a guilt trip on me."

Maggie felt as if she had been assaulted. Her face flushed bright pink. "I don't like you, either!" she flared.

Suddenly Noah was laughing. "You're such a child, Maggie. How someone could live thirty-one years and still behave like a seven-year-old is beyond me."

Dumbfounded at the gall of the man, Maggie stared at him. What he had said was patronizing and infuriating. Yet in his tone there was affection and amusement. She forced herself to speak. "This is all a mistake. I should never have let you talk me into it."

He met her glare, and the laughter died in his eyes. "Don't, Maggie. You'll regret it. I'll get you what you want, and nobody else can promise you that. If you want to keep this strictly business, we will. We'll limit our conversations to the matters at hand. But you've already agreed to our plan."

She turned her back to him. "It's a ridiculous plan."

She felt the grip of his hand on her shoulder as he turned her around again. "Let's stop playing cat and mouse. It doesn't make sense."

Pulling away from him, she recoiled from the anger in his voice. Exhaustion replaced the fury she had felt only a moment ago. All she wanted to do was take two aspirins, go to sleep, and start the day over. He was right, she knew. "Okay," she answered tonelessly. "I'll stop. Do what you have to do. I guess I'll just have to give up any aspirations toward achieving sainthood."

"That's my girl." He took her chin between his thumb and forefinger and lifted her face upward. "Let's get on with it."

Maggie leaned over the heavy glass jeweler's case. All the wedding rings seemed so serious.

"Don't you have one that's sort of frivolous-looking? You know, the kind of ring that says, 'I'm just kidding'?"

"Ma'am?" The bald-headed salesman adjusted his rimless glasses.

"Here, Maggie," Noah called, pointing to a simple, elegant platinum ring. "Try this one."

"Uh-uh," Maggie refused. "That ring is going to see a fiftieth wedding anniversary. I prefer something like that." She indicated a gold ring, which was a series of cut-out triangles strung together by a thin gold band. "It shows that there are some holes in the relationship," she explained. To an obviously exasperated Noah she quickly amended her statement. "I mean, in my head."

"There'll be some holes in your teeth if you don't stop this game." Noah shrugged. "Get that ring if it makes you more comfortable. Hurry, though, because you need to get a wedding dress."

"Wait a minute. Wait just one minute. A ring I can understand, but a dress—no way. Let's not make this more of a farce than we have to."

Casting an embarrassed glance toward the cashier, Noah pulled Maggie toward the corner of the store. "What's the matter with you? You can't talk like that in public. The cashier will hear you."

"Right, and he's going to think we have a lousy relationship and immediately call all the adoption agencies he can think of to tell them not to give us any children."

"Shh. He's looking at us."

"He just thinks we're having a little lovers' quarrel."

"Let's continue this little lovers' quarrel outside, after I pay for the ring," Noah said soothingly.

"Don't you try to patronize me, Noah Jamison. This isn't something little, we're not lovers, and it's not a quarrel. It's a statement of fact. I'm not buying a wedding dress, and I'm not going to wear one, either. The justice of the peace in Saint Paul isn't going to refuse to marry us. Don't worry, I'll wear something appropriate."

"Knowing you, it will probably be a mauve miniskirt with cowboy boots and a Nehru jacket." He impatiently pushed his thick, curly hair back with his hands. "Wait a minute. Did you say a justice of the peace in St. Paul? What's wrong with Minneapolis?" Noah's voice was no longer a whisper.

"I don't want the ceremony to be in Minneapolis. My friends or relatives or colleagues or even just acquaintances might see me."

"Now who's concerned about appearances? Do you really plan to keep this a secret from everyone?"

45

"Well, at least at first." Maggie's tone was suddenly sheepish. "Let's buy the ring."

As they returned to the displays the balding clerk left the back room and approached the counter. "Perhaps you'd like to consider your choice a little longer."

"Choice of rings, you mean?" Maggie probed.

"Yes, of course," the man replied as a slight blush climbed from his cheeks to his pate.

"We'll take the one with the triangular holes in it," said Noah as he grasped Maggie's hand in his.

An impish smile spread over her face. "Aren't we getting a matching one for you?"

"Oh, er, I suppose we are." Noah covered his surprise with a smile that showed most of his teeth. He addressed the clerk. "Do you have one with just the insides of the triangles?"

The clerk answered very seriously, "I'm afraid not, sir. We do have one just like the lady's but in a man's size. Would you like to try it?"

While Noah was having the ring fitted Maggie looked idly out the store's plate-glass window. Shoppers filed past, most of them absorbed in their own thoughts, some of them window-shopping. Just then, one of the passersby caught Maggie's eye and gave her a big grin. Maggie broke out in a sweat. It was a mail clerk who worked at the newspaper. Thankfully he was in no mood to chat. With a wave and the grin still on his face, he hurried past and down the street.

Maggie's heart was still thudding when she rejoined Noah at the counter.

"Guess who I just saw."

"The seven dwarfs."

"Wrong. Ronnie, the mail clerk. I thought I was going to faint. I was sure he was going to come in and talk and see you and the rings and the whole bit and ruin everything."

"Calm down." His voice was gentle. "It's just a couple of rings. We're not buying heroin or dealing in contraband. It's all right. Believe me."

Maggie's laughter trilled nervously. "I bet you think I'm silly."

"I wouldn't use that word." He patted her arm. "Bizarre would be more suitable."

"No-ah! Don't start again."

The clerk cleared his throat. "How will you be paying for the rings, sir?"

"Cash." Noah reached into his pocket.

"I'll pay for mine with a charge card," Maggie cut in.

"Maggie . . ."

Her lips were drawn in a tight line. "It's too soon to start breaking agreements. I'll pay for mine, and you pay for yours."

Noah shrugged helplessly at the clerk. "Women's lib," he explained. Taking out enough cash to cover the cost of his ring, he lay the money on the counter. "I'll wait for you outside, dearest."

As she handed her credit card to the salesclerk, Maggie was careful to avoid his eyes. When he returned it to her with the news that the company had turned down her charge, she quelled a desire to run out of the store. "I don't understand it. I paid the last bill. Oh," she said with a sigh, "it must still be in the mail."

"I'll lay it out," Noah said gruffly, "and you can pay me back later if you insist."

Maggie jumped. "I thought you were outside."

"I came in to see what was taking so long."

"Now you know. Look, why don't we forget this

47

ring thing and buy a couple of fake ones at the five-and-dime?"

"They don't give babies to people with green fingers." Noah smirked.

"Shhh!" Maggie held her finger to her lips. "Do you want the whole world to know?"

Noah took a few big bills from his wallet, tossed them to the clerk, and told him to put the change in the white charity box that sat next to the cash register. Picking up the ring boxes, he slipped them into his pocket, took Maggie's elbow, and steered her out the door.

"We might as well forget it," Maggie stated morosely once out on the sidewalk. "He knows."

"He doesn't know." Noah sounded exasperated. "All he knows is that we're not your typical engaged couple."

"He knows the honeymoon's over," Maggie said dryly. "He's going to tell. Just you wait and see."

"Maggie, you're being bizarre again. Who's he going to tell, and what's he going to tell?"

"It's going to be the headline of tomorrow's *Minneapolis Sentinel.*"

Chuckling, Noah draped his arm over Maggie's shoulders. "Maggie, living with you is going to be a barrel of laughs."

The weight of his arm was heavy on her shoulders. Or maybe, she thought, his arm wasn't heavy, but her entire consciousness was focused on his arm and her shoulders, and she felt that her pores were connecting with his pores and—oh, God—she was being bizarre again, as he would say. Instead of squirming out from under his arm, she rambled on nonsensically, trying to divert her attention. "I don't know about this. In a world where there are mail clerks to see you in jewelry stores and credit card companies to refuse

48

your charges, and cashiers with big ears, can we keep this plan alive and well and living in Minneapolis?"

"His ears didn't have to be too big, the way we were carrying on. Come on, let's stop worrying and have some fun."

"Let's look at baby furniture," Maggie said brightly.

"Let's have some real fun," Noah contradicted.

Maggie folded her arms across her chest. "Fun isn't part of the agreement."

"But it isn't expressly forbidden." Noah chuckled. With cool deliberateness he unfolded her crossed arms and with one hand, he clasped them behind her back at the wrists. With his other hand he lifted her chin upward so that their eyes met. "Is it?"

She couldn't answer right away, for what she read in his eyes unsettled her. It was primitive and male and forceful. It was aggression and desire.

What he read in her eyes pleased him. The flash of defiance could not altogether hide a hint of submission.

Breaking away from him, she curled her hands into fists at her sides. "Don't you ever do that to me again!"

He smiled.

"Oh! You're impossible!"

"Thank you." His steady smile was infuriating.

"Our 'agreement' isn't set in stone, you know," she retorted hotly.

He deliberately misunderstood. "Then we can write 'fun' in."

"Are you playing games with me, or is this a business deal? What's going on here?"

Suddenly, as if her words had just reached him, Noah's entire demeanor became sober. "I was just kidding around. I'm sorry."

A slow smile lit her face. "Do I ever wish I had a tape recorder now!"

Maggie glanced back along the narrow sidewalk and caught a glimpse of the bald cashier staring at them, his nose pressed tightly against the glass of the front window.

CHAPTER FOUR

Something old,
Something new,
Something borrowed,
Something blue.

Her grandmother's pearls; her mother's slip, which she had gone to considerable trouble to borrow; a new dress; and the traditional blue garter fulfilled the criteria. Bizarre. Yep, she thought, that was her. Good old bizarre Maggie. Why in heaven's name she should be borrowing slips and buying garters was beyond her. Why she had bought a new outfit was especially hard to understand. True, it was a beige suit and not a wedding dress, but she had still partially given in to Noah. She just didn't know! The distinction between playacting and real life was getting harder and harder to discern.

Maggie grabbed her stomach. Butterflies, she thought, although they felt more like tadpoles tumbling playfully about her insides. She was actually going through with this venture. She'd taken the day, October nineteenth, off from work, told her mother she was going away with friends for the weekend, and told her friends she'd be visiting her mother and relatives for a few days. She'd have time to move some of her stuff to Noah's rented house and set up

51

housekeeping with her—her mind recoiled at the word—with her *husband*.

When her doubts threatened to overcome her, she flipped through a magazine aimed at new adoptive parents. The smiling children and upbeat stories quashed her doubts. She hurriedly dressed, assembled her papers, and called Noah. If she moved fast enough, she wouldn't be able to think, and things often went better without thought.

"Hello, Noah."

She was greeted by Noah's recorded message. "This is Noah. I can't answer your call right now, but if you'll leave your name and number at the sound of the tone, I'll get back to you as soon as possible, unless, of course, you're someone I don't wish to speak to."

Maggie duly waited for the tone. "Your message is a little off-putting, dear and—"

"Maggie, Maggie, calm down. I just turned the machine on because I didn't want to explain anything to anyone. Believe it or not, I'm nervous."

"You are?" Maggie's tone softened at Noah's uncharacteristic admission.

"Yeah, I've got a column due Monday, and I haven't even begun to write it." He paused. "Wait, don't hang up. I was only kidding."

"Please don't kid. I'm nervous enough as it is. I'll meet you at the courthouse in St. Paul. I can't wait around here anymore or I'll bust."

"Suit yourself, Mrs. Jamison. We're due there by nine-thirty."

"I'll be there. Don't worry." Maggie hung up and toyed with the words *Mrs. Jamison*. She liked their sound but resented Noah's using them so fliply. Then she remembered not to think and soon found herself listening mindlessly to soothing pop songs on her radio. When an old rock 'n' roll song came on the air with the lyrics "goin' to the chapel and we're gonna get married . . . goin' to the chapel of love," Maggie jumped up and shut the radio off. Leaning against her kitchen sink, she found that she was crying. Wasn't this supposed to be the happiest day of her life? But, no, that would be reality. This was fantasy. Or maybe that was fantasy and this was reality. Confused, she shook her head. Whether it was reality or fantasy, it was getting late and she did have an appointment to get married.

Finding a metered parking spot directly across from the courthouse, Maggie reached room 409 at nine-fifteen.

Noah was not there yet, so Maggie did what she imagined anyone in her situation would do. Looking very much the nervous bride, she paced up and down the corridor. Her eyes downcast, she felt after a few minutes that she knew every crack and stain of the courthouse floor.

" 'Scuse me, ma'am."

Maggie whirled around to come face-to-face with a gangly, crew-cut, ruddy-faced young man holding a gray hat in his hand. "Yes?"

"I think I'm s'posed to be meetin' you here."

"You are?"

"Yes, ma'am. You here to get married?"

Her blood pressure rose as her heart sank. Noah hadn't the gall to send a proxy in his place, had he?

"You my bride?" the man persisted. "I'm s'posed to be meetin' my bride here. You the one I picked out, ain't ya? You a mite prettier than your picture in the catalogue. Yes, sir, you little pixie. But I'd a-knowed you anywheres."

Maggie heard muffled laughter behind her. She turned, and there was Noah Jamison, trying his

53

darnedest to keep from rolling on the floor with laughter. "S-sorry, fella, you've got the wrong girl!" He had a brief coughing spell, which Maggie suspected was a cover-up for his laughter. "But I must compliment you on your good taste. If I saw the lady's picture in a catalogue, I'd ask her to marry me myself."

At a total loss for words, Maggie just scowled. She didn't protest, however, when Noah led her back down the hall and into room 409.

"Had yourself a little adventure, huh?" Noah kidded.

Maggie shrugged. "I'm loath to say that what that boy is doing, ordering a mail-order bride, is not qualitatively different from what we're doing."

"Then why say it? Anyway, you're wrong. The motivations are different. We're motivated by unselfishness, and that boy is motivated by hormones. He's probably from one of those small towns up north. And you know what Minnesota winters do to hormones!"

"And what do they do to common sense?"

"Come on, Maggie, not on our wedding day. You've got a whole marriage in front of you to whine and complain and make nasty insinuations."

Maggie's words fairly exploded from her. "That's it! It's off! I'm not going to go through with this farce. Find yourself a mail-order bride, preferably one who can't speak."

Maggie turned on her heels and ran smack into the young man from northern Minnesota, knocking him flat on his back.

"You really are a mighty powerful little lady." He looked up groggily from the hard tile floor. "If you'd like to reconsider my offer, I'd be pleased to make you my missus, catalogue or no catalogue."

54

"I'm sorry, sir. Noah, help the man to his feet, will you?"

Noah offered him a hand. "Are you okay? I'm Noah Jamison, and this is my fiancée, Maggie Clay."

The man nodded, introduced himself, and then spotted his bride, a pleasant, shyly smiling Asian woman. Maggie, her anger dissipated by the incident, wondered how anyone could mistake her for the woman.

Reading Maggie's thoughts, Noah winked at her, then grasped her elbow and guided her toward room 409. "We're all a little nervous," he assured her gently.

"I guess so," she admitted. Noah stopped and looked down at her. Hesitating for a second, he turned and said in a hearty tone to the other couple, "Come and join us. Let's have a double wedding. We've got a lot in common. And, if you don't mind, I'd like to pick up the fee. We'll say it's by way of apology for that spill you took."

"That's mighty friendly of you folks. Cujo and I right appreciate that," the man replied with a big grin.

All four of them entered the chambers in room 409, the young man and Cujo chattering to each other in broken English, Maggie and Noah quiet. After a few moments of silence Noah remarked, "Why so quiet, Maggie? We're both quiet as church mice."

"You mean courthouse mice, don't you?" Maggie's smile took the sting out of her words.

The appropriate forms having been filled out, Maggie found herself slightly dazed as she stood in front of a kindly, gray-haired old judge. Why wasn't she at work? Why was Noah Jamison holding her elbow and smiling? Why was this strange couple giggling beside her? Once again she put herself on automatic pilot and flew blind.

The next thing she knew, she heard the judge saying, "You may now kiss the brides." She realized with a start that they were married, that she had already said "I do," and that she was about to kiss her new husband for the first time in her life. She felt dizzy.

As Noah bent to kiss her she noticed a concerned look in his eyes. The last thing she remembered before passing out was the young man from northern Minnesota yelling, "Whoopee, whoopee, I've got myself a little wifey!"

Coming to a few minutes later in the judge's private chamber, Maggie was relieved to be alone with Noah. Cujo and her new husband happily had disappeared. "What happened?" she murmured.

"You fainted," Noah told her. "You must have swooned from the power of my kiss. Take it easy for a while so our friends have a chance to get out of here before we do. Otherwise they might become the first couple to be our friends." He spoke with a wry tilt to his head and a warm expression in his eyes. Maggie felt a surge of fondness for him.

"How could I have fainted? I never fainted before in my life."

"Well . . ." His voice trailed off. "I never kissed you before. Do you feel all right?"

"I'm fine now that that incredible, super powerful, faint-inducing kiss is behind me. Just a little shaken. Well, at least I fainted after saying 'I do' and not before." She paused to think. "Whoopee!" She laughed. "Did you ever hear anyone yell 'whoopee' when they were married?" She kept laughing, more out of leftover anxiety than anything else.

"Come on, Mrs. Jamison. It's time to go home." Linking arms, they walked out into the corridor.

"What did the judge do when I fainted?" she asked, feeling relieved that the ceremony was now behind them.

"He didn't do anything. I think he was half asleep. I'm glad he didn't recognize me. I once did a series of columns on incompetent judges and cited his falling asleep during criminal trials as one of my examples. It's one of the reasons he's now conducting marriage ceremonies instead of robbery trials."

"What did he say, though? He must have said something," Maggie asked curiously.

"He just kept repeating, 'Twenty years with no chance for parole, twenty years with no chance for parole.'"

Maggie giggled as she swung her tiny black purse at him. "Maybe no parole, but he didn't say anything about jailbreaks." She sprinted away from him, weaving her way through the milling lawyers, clients, and families. Just as she was approaching the wide columns that straddled the door to the courthouse, Noah's strong hand wrapped itself around her wrist.

He pulled her to him and relinked their arms. "There are such things as wardens, you know." His eyes twinkled. She looked so sweet and vulnerable, he thought. He ached to touch her, to stroke her slender neck, to caress her shoulders, to kiss her breasts. Despite the anticlimactic fainting spell that had seized her, his lips recalled the feel of her lips as he kissed her. They were soft and yielding, pliant and feminine. He felt the blood rushing through his veins and wondered, not for the first time, about the wisdom of this business arrangement.

Clearing her throat, Maggie wished that he would stop looking at her that way. It made her skin feel warm and tingly and made her heart thud painfully in her chest. This was a purely chemical reaction, she told herself. Or maybe an animal reaction. But it had nothing to do with Noah, the man. Nothing!

Noah swallowed. This was crazy. He had to break the spell. "How about a little celebration? Let's go break open a bottle of champagne."

"Champagne?" Maggie wrinkled her nose. "That's for real weddings. Anyway, I never drink during the day. How about some cheesecake?"

"You mean photos? You want to go and be photographed jumping out of a wedding cake wearing only a few tassles?"

Maggie grimaced. "Let's go to Becky's Cafeteria. They have the best cheesecake in the Twin Cities."

"You want to celebrate your wedding in a cafeteria?" Noah acted incredulous.

Maggie ran her hand over her eyes. "Don't make more of a parody out of this than it already is."

"Once you lose your sense of humor, my dear, you've lost everything." Maggie certainly knew how to wreck someone's good mood, he thought, but maybe she was right.

Having agreed to meet outside Becky's Cafeteria, Noah and Maggie each drove their own car from St. Paul to the area in Minneapolis that boasted some of the nation's finest art centers, theaters, and concert halls. Maggie found a parking spot just behind Noah's car, a block from the cafeteria.

Becky's Cafeteria was a chic after-theater spot furnished with antique furniture, lace curtains, and oil paintings.

"I always feel like I'm sitting in my grandmother's parlor when I come here," Noah remarked.

"Me, too, even though my grandmother never had a parlor like this," Maggie whispered. "And I always feel like I should whisper." Heading for the front of the cafeteria line in the back room, Maggie groaned. "You're not going to believe this but . . ."

"I know. They're out of cheesecake."

"How did you guess?"

Noah considered for a moment. "On a day when your bride faints, of course there won't be cheese-cake,"

"Of course there won't be cheesecake," Maggie repeated. "Want to run that by me again? No, don't. Let's have apple pie. Do you like apple pie?"

Maggie picked up two dishes of apple pie, a cup of coffee, a glass of milk, and deposited them on their trays. Moving quickly to the cash register, she took out two dollar bills for her pie.

"Maggie, put that money away." Noah's voice was sharp.

"Remember the terms. . . ."

"It's my wedding present to you," Noah cut in impatiently as he handed four dollars to the cashier and waited for his change.

"I'll buy the next time," Maggie muttered through clenched teeth.

"Why don't you buy me a year's supply of Alka Seltzer? Something tells me I'm going to need it."

"Noah!" Maggie's tone was hurt.

Noah grinned. "Sorry. That was no way to talk to my bride on our wedding day. Let's make a toast."

"With your milk and my coffee or the apple pie?" Maggie demanded.

He held up his milk glass. "To . . ." He paused. "Our success."

As they clinked cup and glass Maggie was struck by his eyes. They were lighter than usual, with gold flecks dancing around the pupils.

"You have beautiful eyes," Maggie remarked, and then, as if realizing that her remark might be miscon-

59

strued, she added, "Now, my best feature is my bone structure. Isn't it remarkable how you can always find something beautiful about someone?"

Noah laughed. "I don't quite know how to answer you. You compliment me, then you insult me, then you leave a remarkable opening for me to do the same to you, all immediately after you marry me. You're an interesting woman, Maggie Jamison."

Putting down her cup abruptly, Maggie spilled several drops of coffee on her new suit. "Darn!" she exclaimed as she brushed at the slowly spreading stain. "What did you call me?"

"Maggie."

"No, after Maggie," she insisted as she rubbed at the linen with a wet napkin.

"Jamison. You see, when two people get married, it's customary for the wife to take the husband's last name." He spoke patiently as if he were explaining something to a child.

"Noah." Maggie used the same patient tone. "I don't want to disillusion you, but you, uh, whoopee, have not gotten yourself a little wifey. You have a business partner, and I would appreciate it if you would confine your jokes to neutral matters." Maggie kept rubbing at her suit.

Noah blinked as if he hadn't heard. "You're making a mess of your suit."

Looking down at her lap, Maggie was confronted with a large coffee stain in a wet mess of linen. "By trying to make it better, I just made it worse." She lifted her eyes to him meaningfully.

"Come on, let's go home. I've got some excellent stain remover there."

"Home?"

"Yeah, you know the place where Mr. and Mrs. Jamison live. The modest split level on the respect-

60

able street. It's the one the social workers will say is perfect for two children." His voice grew more somber. "I'm not going to have to fight you every step of the way, I hope."

Covering her eyes with one hand, Maggie shook her head. "I'm sorry."

"You're beautiful when you're contrite." Smiling, Noah removed her hand from her eyes and held it for a moment. He thought how small and fragile her hand was and how he must take care, for with one unthinking squeeze he could fracture some bones. Her hand was like her. She, too, was fragile, though she pretended not to be. As he could break her hand, so, too, could he break the woman.

She pretended to be so callous and hard and untouchable when in fact he knew she was attracted to him. He read it in her eyes. He would have to take care with her. Keep their relationship light. Lots of kidding around. He would have to control his urges. If she only knew how he wanted to make love to her! He bet she was a tiger in bed. Or maybe a kitten. It didn't matter. He would take her either way. Gladly.

Gently removing her hand from his, he thought how tough this year was going to be. If he wasn't careful, she would end up hurt and miserable. He was in the market for a child, not for a real wife. Noah could handle the situation, though. He had had lots of women. But Maggie—well, he couldn't be sure about her. Oh, he knew she wasn't a virgin. But still, she seemed somehow naive and inexperienced. Keep it light, buddy, he said to himself.

To her he said, "Maggie, ol' girl, we can't let that stain set in your suit. Don't want the day to be a total loss now, do we? By the way, did I tell you what a pretty suit you're wearing?"

Maggie laughed. "I think you care more about my

suit than I do. But okay. I suppose we should go over to the house and decide which space is whose, if you know what I mean."

"I think I do, and I'll tell you what—whoever gets there first gets to choose the color scheme for the bathroom."

Maggie smiled. "You win by default. I'm a slow driver, and I don't care what color the bathroom is. But, anyway, I'll meet you there."

As Maggie drove the twenty-five minutes it took to get from Minneapolis Center to Brooklyn Park, she didn't notice the lakes or the trees. She didn't notice the driver who almost side-swiped her, nor the red light she almost didn't make. She was lost in thought. She thought that Noah had the broadest shoulders and the tenderest smile she had seen in a long time. She thought of how she liked the rough, padded feel of his hand when he held hers. She thought about the look on his face when she opened her eyes after her brief faint and how the fear had been replaced by relief. She thought about his chest. She wondered if it was hairy. And then she decided to stop thinking.

In his rearview mirror Noah saw Maggie as she almost went through a red light and as she narrowly escaped an accident. He shook his head. That lady had better improve her driving or he would permanently short-circuit her battery!

With no more of Maggie's escapades to occupy him, he returned to his own line of thought. What Noah couldn't tolerate, even in himself, was dishonesty. As he caught glimpses of Maggie's blond head in his mirror, he realized that maybe he hadn't been showing a whole lot of integrity.

After all, he knew he didn't really want a wife. What he wanted was a child and a full-time housekeeper. But a wife—forget it! Having come this far without the embroilments of the hopelessly archaic institution of marriage, he wasn't going to fall into the trap at this stage of the game.

Lost in their respective reveries, Maggie's and Noah's trips to their suburban paradise seemed to take no time at all.

Maggie pulled up into the driveway next to Noah's car.

"Well, here we are," Noah called out to an uncertain-looking Maggie. "One thing I'm going to do that's traditional"—he paused and grinned wickedly—"is carry my new bride over the threshold." Swooping her up in his strong arms before she had a chance to protest, Noah strode to the front door, kicked it open, and, with a full-bodied laugh, deposited Maggie in the living room.

"You not Tarzan. Me not Jane," Maggie commented dryly.

"Me already know that. Look around. Make yourself at home."

Maggie nodded. "I suppose the first thing I ought to do is give you a check for the first month's rent. What do I owe you?"

"Ah . . ."

"I'm giving you half the rent. Don't try any funny stuff like telling me it's less than it is."

"Four hundred and fifty."

"Okay." Tearing a check out of her checkbook, Maggie began writing. "I'll make that out for two hundred and twenty-five dollars, then. Even steven."

He surveyed her determined stance and then drawled, "If it's even steven you want, then you owe me four hundred and fifty. The rent is nine hundred dollars a month."

Her eyes flew open. "Nine—" Silent for a moment, she did some quick figuring in her head. With that kind of rent and her loft she would barely be able to make it. Recovering, she tore up her first check and began writing a second one. "It's a bit high, don't you think?"

His eyebrows were raised quizzically. "That's the price of bananas, kiddo. We want to make a good impression on the people from the adoption agencies. This is a solid neighborhood. It's got everything: well-kept lawns, well-fed children, and Tupperware parties. Your neighborhood, on the other hand . . ."

"I get the picture," Maggie conceded with a small sigh as she tossed the hair out of her eyes.

"Maggie." He grabbed the wrist that held the pen and slid his hand down to the juncture of her thumb and forefinger. Lightly caressing the smooth flesh, as if he had forgotten his resolve to be casual, he repeated her name. "Maggie."

She had a momentary feeling of panic. Then her instincts told her to pull away from him. Her voice was icy. "What is it?"

Creasing his forehead into a frown, Noah seemed suddenly to come to his senses. He laughed. "Sorry." He held up his hands as if to a law officer. "I won't touch you again. It's just that this isn't going to be easy for either of us, so I don't see why you insist on putting yourself under financial strain as well. The money doesn't mean anything to me. I've got plenty of it."

She heard the superiority behind his words and gritted her teeth. "Your offer is kind, but please don't make it again. I will not accept." With cool deliberation she finished writing out the check, tore it off, and handed it to him.

Taking it, he was careful to touch only the check. "She who makes the rules lives with them."

"If you ever get tired of writing newspaper columns, you can write the insides of fortune cookies," she said with a small grin. "Anyway, who ever heard of a newspaper columnist who won't miss nine hundred dollars?"

"I've got other sources of income."

"Oh, ho! Illegal or immoral?"

"Unfortunately, neither. Just some very dull and very lucrative real estate holdings."

"So why aren't we living in one of your holdings?"

"Because they're office buildings. That would look even worse than your warehouse!"

"Appearances, appearances." She laughed. "Well, for all appearances we're an old, married couple of two and a half hours. So, if you don't mind, I'd like to examine my bedroom. Shall we toss for the master bedroom? The nursery will be the middle room and the bedroom on the end will be for the loser."

"We're both winners," he said grimly, "and you can have the master bedroom."

"It's not necessary," she put in quickly. "You can have it. I won't really be sleeping here."

"Like hell you won't. You'll have to sleep here. What will the neighbors say?"

"They're not going to do a bed check!"

"You'd be surprised at what the neighbors know," he said with laughter twinkling in his eyes. "They'll come in and scold if we don't brush after every meal and if you forget to brush those golden tresses one night." He gestured toward her hair.

"Oh, you!" She laughed uncomfortably, for she had the sudden impression that he would have liked to run his hands through her hair. Or maybe it was that she would have liked to run hers through his dark, thick curls. "Next thing you'll be telling me is that we have to share the same bed because of the neighbors."

"You said it, not me." He grinned diabolically.

Not even deigning to dignify his response with a look over her shoulder, Maggie headed off for an inspection of the rooms. She was grateful to see that Noah had furnished the third bedroom with a sofa bed and a desk, making it resemble a study more than a bedroom. The nursery had been left empty.

"I figured we'd furnish the babies' room together," he explained. "Why don't you go on in and take a look at your bedroom?" Leading the way, he flung open the door. At the foot of the double bed stood a small folding table graced by an enormous bouquet of white roses.

"Those are lovely," Maggie said, gasping. "I've never seen so many white roses in my life. There must be five dozen there. But why?"

"A housewarming present," he answered quietly. "That's all."

Dropping the purse she still carried onto the bed, Maggie buried her nose in the delicate scent of the flowers. When she looked up, she caught a glimpse of the shy, yet unmistakably triumphant smile playing around Noah's lips. She felt oddly afraid.

CHAPTER FIVE

"Maggie, where's the shampoo?" Noah wandered into the living room dripping wet, wearing nothing but a towel wrapped around his waist.

"How should I know?" My God! she thought, jolted by the effect his seminudity had upon her. Her eyes were fastened on the covering of black curls upon his broad chest. Her palms suddenly felt moist and her knees weak as she studied the broad expanse of bronze skin stretched over hard muscle. She had had no idea that his physique, with its powerful shoulders and solid arms, his sinewy neck and tapered waist, would be so dashingly beautiful. She forced herself to look away.

"I'm freezing and I can't find the shampoo." He shivered.

"Maybe you didn't buy any," she answered with studied unconcern.

He stood right in front of her so that her eyes were level with his pectorals. "I bought it. You probably didn't unpack it."

"Gee," she taunted him, hoping he hadn't noticed her sharp intake of breath.

"Why don't you get organized, Maggie? This house is a mess—clothes all over the place, papers. The breakfast dishes aren't even washed."

His words penetrated. For the next ominously silent minute Maggie did a slow burn. "So wash them."

"I don't wash dishes," he announced imperiously.

"Well, neither do I."

"Well, you'd better," he warned.

"Oh, yeah?"

"Yeah."

"So divorce me." She didn't know whether she felt like laughing or shouting.

"Maybe I'll just stop shoveling the snow." Noah paused, quirked one eyebrow, then laughed. "We had better stop this bickering. We're behaving like real married people."

An amused smile curved her lips. "So this is what the real thing is like. No wonder I never succumbed! I hear that compromise is a widely used technique in marriage. Therefore, I vote for paper plates from now on. In any case, how are the adoption procedures going? I haven't had a chance to talk to you about it over the last few days."

Noah looked down at the goose bumps that had risen on his flesh. "Do you think maybe we could postpone this discussion—at least until I rinse off the soap?"

"Of course," Maggie responded airily as Noah turned toward the bathroom. "By the way, I'll bet you didn't look under the sink. If you do, you'll probably find some shampoo."

Before entering the steamy bathroom, Noah turned to glare at her, but it was a glare softened by affection, Maggie thought.

In the couple of months that had transpired since the start of their arrangement, Maggie's and Noah's paths had crossed only a few times. When one was on the way in, the other was on the way out. Communication between them was accomplished mostly by means of notes left on the kitchen counter. Whether this was by design or coincidence, Maggie had not yet decided.

What she did know for certain was that after the shampoo incident she preferred Noah's notes to the flesh-and-blood man. Things would have been okay had not the strain of keeping up two households turned into a budgetary nightmare beyond her worst expectations. When doing her original calculations, she had not figured in the cost of utilities in their electrically heated and poorly insulated Brooklyn Park house. The winter dragged on interminably. The days and nights were long, dreary, and bitter cold. To Noah's pleas that she let him, if not pay a greater share, at least loan her the money, she consistently turned a deaf ear. She would manage somehow.

The sounds of cutlery being washed and Noah's implacably cheerful humming began to wear on Maggie's nerves. Slumped on the rented Danish-style sofa, Maggie regretted that she had permitted Noah to convince her to eat dinner with him in the house. Avoidance of him had begun to be a habit with which she had grown comfortable.

But Noah had said they had to talk and that they should start spending time together in order to learn more about each other. He said that they should go out together, do things, be seen. Maggie grudgingly acquiesced but had refused his offer to make dinner for the two of them. He could make his, and she would make hers.

"You don't mind if I set the table for you, do you?" Noah's voice floated out from the kitchen.

"I don't need a knife and fork," Maggie answered brusquely.

"Oh, you just want a spoon. What are you making for yourself, bouillabaisse?"

Maggie detected the ironic note in his voice and deliberately ignored it. Her tone was all sweetness and light. "Oh, no. I wouldn't eat fish stew if you paid me. Perhaps I haven't told you that I've become a vegetarian?" Far be it from her, she thought angrily, to tell him the reason for it—that she could no longer afford fish or meat. All she had been eating lately was peanut butter, cream cheese, macaroni, and vitamin pills. If he wouldn't keep the thermostat turned up so darned high, she might be able to buy herself a hamburger a couple of times a week.

Noah's footsteps sounded from behind her. Picking up the magazine that lay on her lap, Maggie pretended to read.

"I think we'll eat in the dining room tonight. The kitchen is kind of stuffy and, well, this is our first dinner at home."

"Big deal," Maggie muttered.

"What?"

"Cut it out," Maggie elaborated.

"Temper, temper," Noah teased. "I think you're suffering from meat withdrawal. How about sharing my nice juicy steak with me?"

"Not on your nice juicy life."

Noah laughed and proceeded to hum his song; Maggie thought it was something from a Broadway show, maybe *Cats*. With grating good humor he brought out a white linen tablecloth, matching napkins, bone china dishes (Maggie had been making do with paper plates) and (she thought about hiring a contract killer) a bouquet of fresh flowers for the centerpiece.

Standing back to survey his handiwork, he wore a smug expression. "I set a nice table, if I do say so myself."

Craning her neck from her position on the sofa, Maggie feigned agreement. "The flowers are pretty."

"They're in celebration of our three-month anniversary."

Maggie swallowed. "I hadn't noticed."

"Liar. Happy anniversary, dear." He picked out a red zinnia and strode into the living area of the L-shaped room. Before Maggie's brain could process his words, he had bent down in front of her and was placing the flower behind her ear.

Unsure of the measure of sarcasm behind his words, Maggie remained still. His face was very near to hers, and she caught the fresh scent of his aftershave and felt the rough wool of his sweater.

"Are you trying to impersonate a wooden Indian or something?"

"I'm sorry. The flower is very lovely. Thank you, Noah." Maggie felt uncomfortable, feeling the beauty of the simple gesture yet not willing to respond to it.

"What is this? The flower is very lovely. Thank you, Noah. You don't talk like that." His tone was gently mocking. "Are you feeling all right, Maggie?" Noah stood and squinted down at her. "Come on. Let's eat. I think your blood sugar is low or something."

Maggie followed him into the never-used dining room and was struck by the simple elegance of the table he had set. Two large candles were set on either side of the flower arrangement. Clear, crystal water glasses were placed next to smaller wine goblets. The white china was so fine, it was translucent. He flicked

71

off the light switch so that the warm glow of candle-light filled the dining room.

"You sit down and I'll bring in the food." The odor of broiling steak spiced with garlic wafted in.

Maggie swallowed. At that moment there was nothing she craved so much as a good steak. "Bring in your food. I haven't even made my dinner yet."

He held up his hand. "Sit. I'll fix it for you. I have an inkling of what you have in mind."

Obediently Maggie sat at one end of the table with her hands folded primly on her lap. She had visions of herself diving on top of his steak and burying her teeth into the red meat. Perhaps she ought to recite a mantra, maybe the syllable *om*. It was all a question of mind over matter or for her, she thought ruefully, of mantra over meat.

As she sat there listening to Noah's puttering in the kitchen, she half-expected (half-hoped?) that he would come out with two steaks. Maybe she would allow her objections to be overcome just this once.

She couldn't suppress the joy that bubbled up in her throat and the hunger pangs that squeezed her insides as he came into the dining room carrying a tray laden with two covered silver serving dishes of the same size. She shook her head in disgust at her own feelings of anticipation. That the thought of a steak should make her so happy was positively decadent.

Carefully Noah lay one platter to Maggie's left and the other to the right of his chair. Midway between them he lay a tray of scallions and raw vegetables.

Maggie could have hugged him. Scallions and steak! Unclasping her hands, she placed the linen napkin on her lap. She watched as Noah made a last quick trip to the kitchen and returned with two decanters of wine. The one containing a darker, red

72

wine he placed near him; the other he placed nearer to Maggie.

"Well"—he smiled at her—"shall we begin?" He poured his glass full of wine and asked Maggie if she would like him to pour for her. She shook her head. Very slowly Noah uncovered his dinner. A large, bloody steak imperiously took up the entire platter. With the aroma of fine, aged beef filling the dining room, Maggie could no longer pretend nonchalance. Eagerly she uncovered her own platter. She stared.

There sat a lone sandwich, peanut butter and grape jelly spilling over the sides and oozing through the porous white bread. Noah's two thumbprints, clearly visible on the upper slice of bread, seemed to taunt her.

Slowly she raised her glance to meet Noah's laughing eyes. With fork and steak knife poised in the air he nodded briskly, *"Bon appétit."*

"You too," she managed to answer as she reached for the decanter Noah had strategically placed beside her plate. Maybe if she drank enough wine, she would forget what she was eating. Filling her glass to the halfway mark, she thought that its clear color indicated a young, fruity wine. She held out her glass in a pantomime of a toast and took a long swallow.

Cranberry-apple juice! He had filled her decanter with cranberry-apple juice! She thought fleetingly that murder was too good for him.

Noah's chin dripped with steak juice. Gnashing her teeth, Maggie bit into her sandwich. Her tongue stuck to the roof of her mouth, and she sought relief with another sip of the juice.

"A very nice, hardy wine," Noah remarked as he held his goblet up to the light. "Perfect for a New York strip steak." He smacked his lips. "You vegetarians don't know what you're missing. But," he said,

73

waxing philosophical, "I admire your strength of character. I certainly know that I could never eat a peanut butter and jelly sandwich while my mate was feasting on a tender piece of beef. Peanut butter was what you wanted, wasn't it?" He arched his eyebrows innocently. "I looked in the refrigerator and that's all you had. I see you don't indulge in the fruit of the vine either, except in its nonfermented state. Very admirable, indeed. I'm sure the social worker will be impressed."

Not knowing what to do or say, Maggie took another bite of her sandwich. Noah jumped up at the sound of the oven timer. "Oh, the potatoes are finished. I let them go a little longer." A second later he poked his head back into the dining room. "Is your sandwich all right? Does it need more jelly?"

Deciding to go along with his little game, Maggie answered that she did need more, but that she didn't want any peanut butter on this one and preferred the new raspberry jam she had just bought rather than the grape jelly he had used on her sandwich. Even people without money could enjoy the best jams. While he was in the kitchen Maggie took advantage of his temporary absence to shamelessly ogle his steak. "Also I'd like the bread toasted if you don't mind." At least she could make him work a little at his game, she figured.

"Anything else?"

"Yes, could you bring me a glass of my skim milk? The juice with the jam is a mite too sweet."

"Aye, aye, ma'am."

Feeling that she had scored a small victory, Maggie resolved to make it through the dinner without letting Noah get to her. His little prank would fail if she didn't acknowledge it.

Noah pranced back in a few moments later with a

74

waiter's tray on which were steaming platters of roast potatoes and buttered broccoli, a Caesar salad, a tall glass of milk, and a raspberry jam sandwich on toast.

"I heard that they're expanding the Sunday book review section at the *Tribune*." Maggie's tone was relentlessly matter-of-fact. "It seems like Mavis Palmer's really getting her way. More than half the books reviewed are by women, and the reviewers usually are too."

Noah couldn't respond at first since, Maggie guessed, he made it a point to keep his mouth full as much of the time as possible. Maggie began to fear that she would become hypnotized by the incessant movement of fork to plate to mouth and by the inexorable bobbing of his Adam's apple.

"Mavis Palmer won't last long," he said finally. "Every time some woman author with a hormonal imbalance writes a book about menopause, she carries on as if it's the new *War and Peace*."

Maggie gasped. "Why, you—"

Noah held up a hand. "Just joking." He grinned at her from across the table. "Mmm. Terrific steak."

Taking a small bite of her sandwich, Maggie chewed slowly. When she swallowed, the food caught in her throat. She gulped her milk to wash it down, but she could still feel it lying there, dry and lumpy. There was no sound at the table save for the clinking of glass as it was set down upon the table, of fork against plate, and of a knife slicing through thick meat. What had first appeared to her to be total silence now seemed a cacophony of sound.

Crossing and then uncrossing her legs, Maggie shifted in her chair. "So! You said we had to talk!"

"Mm hmm," Noah replied with the air of a man who hasn't a care in the world. "Great steak."

75

Maggie slammed her sandwich onto her plate. "You said that already! Presumably you've got me sitting here watching you stuff yourself for some weightier conversation than 'great steak.'"

Carefully balancing utensils along the edge of his plate, Noah set his forearms on the table and leaned forward. "We haven't seen much of each other since that little to-do we had about the shampoo and the housecleaning."

Maggie picked up a crumb of white bread and rolled it between her fingers. "That's our strategy, divide and conquer—divide us and conquer the adoption agency. If we saw each other much more than ten minutes a week, I think we'd divide and conquer ourselves!" Though she meant it to be ironic, she realized as soon as the words were out of her mouth that he might misunderstand.

He did. "We should let down our defenses, you mean. Try being friends—or even more. I've considered that alternative myself. I'm not so sure it would work, but the idea is tempting. You must realize that you're a very attractive woman and I'm a normal man."

Maggie tried to keep her voice at a civilized level. "First you give me peanut butter. Then you give me cranberry-apple juice. Then you give me jam. And to top it all off"—she flashed a saccharine smile—"you give me a stomachache. I think we had better stick to leaving each other notes on the kitchen counter."

"This is going to be much too complicated to handle with notes left on the kitchen counter, Maggie."

"All right, we'll leave them on the refrigerator, then."

"Funny girl. Listen, I've talked to my doctor friend, and he's going to write additional letters for us attesting to our inability to conceive a child to-

gether and attesting to our suitability as parents."
Noah rose and began to clear the table.

Maggie grimaced. "I want you to know I feel very uncomfortable with this. It's lying. I don't like lying." She spoke in a rapid, nervous staccato. "I've never lied like this before."

"It's not lying. It's just stretching the truth a bit."

"What do you mean, stretching the truth a bit?" She rolled her eyes toward the ceiling. "That's just a wormy way to say lying." She carried her plates to the kitchen and returned to find Noah pacing the dining room and gesturing.

"Listen, we can't conceive a child together because in order to do that it's necessary to sleep together and we don't. So you see, we're not lying. We're just omitting certain truths." He creased his forehead and scratched his temple. "Is that your objection to sleeping with me? You don't want to be a liar?"

"Noah, you're a horse's ass, and *that's* my objection to sleeping with you."

He held his hand to his heart. "I'm stricken. You've mortally wounded me. But you know what?" His voice softened. "I don't believe you. I'd prove it to you too"—his eyes raked her from head to toe—"but there are other things we have to worry about first."

Maggie was humiliated by the hot flush she knew was suffusing her cheeks with color. "I'm not interested in your proof. What other problems? What are you talking about now, Noah?"

Noah was matter-of-fact. "Documents alone aren't going to convince any social worker that they should give us babies. We also have to learn to interact with each other."

"Interact?" she looked askance. "Don't you mean act? We have to put on a good act."

"If you like." His voice was bland. "We have to learn about each other, our habits, our likes and dislikes. Maybe one of us is a bed wetter and we don't know it."

"Well, then, the social worker won't know it, either," Maggie said sensibly. "Look, I agree that we have to sit down and decide how we're going to present ourselves, but that shouldn't take very long, not more than a couple of serious hours."

"Wrong, my dear. It's going to take lots of time, some of it serious, some not so serious. Let's not get cocky about this. Social workers aren't idiots. It's bad enough that we're not really husband and wife. We shouldn't also be strangers. If you hand me a cup of tea right after I've said that I never drink the stuff, things are going to look fishy."

Maggie paced to the end of the room and back again. "I suppose if we've gone this far, we ought to do the thing right."

Noah nodded, all business now. "We're going to have to go through a program of total immersion. No more running back and forth between homes, Maggie. You'll have to move in completely, and we'll have to see each other every day. I mean, every morning and every evening. I started a subscription to the *Star* and the *Tribune* so that I can pick it up off the lawn every morning, and when we go off to work, I expect a wifely good-bye kiss. We'll have dinner together at night and even invite the neighbors in. We can have a cocktail party. You can learn to play bridge. We can have people in for cards, and I'll start playing racquetball with some of the neighborhood guys."

"Ah! Conjugal bliss." Maggie smiled ironically.

Noah frowned at her. "And now for the good news!"

Maggie's eyes twinkled mischievously. "You're a husband who cheats, and you'll be spending most of your time with your mistress!"

Noah's face mirrored his impatience. "Must you always be so sarcastic? You must be protecting a mighty vulnerable lady with all that heavy-duty barbed wire you have wrapped around yourself."

The blood drained from her face. Maggie stared at him. Could he know that every time he looked her way her heart did double time? Could he know that in bed at night she often imagined his face before drifting off to sleep? Could he know that if they hadn't had this very delicate business arrangement and this commitment to live together for a year, she most probably would have made love to him already? "There's a reason turtles have shells and porcupines quills. It's to protect against predators."

"And I'm the predator?" He laughed.

"Well, you ain't the turtle." She smiled at him. "So! What's that good news you were threatening me with?" she asked, trying to sound casual.

Placing his hands on her shoulders, Noah smiled down at her. "You're incorrigible. The good news, my friend, is that we have an appointment with the social worker from the Sweet Care Agency."

Maggie gasped. "When?"

"Exactly six weeks from today."

"Oh, that's wonderful!" Unable to help herself, she wound her hands partway around his upper arms and squeezed. Or tried to. It ended up, she thought, looking more like a tribute to his bulging muscles than an enthusiastic squeeze. "How did you wangle the interview so fast?"

"Chalk it up to charm and know-how."

"Modesty, thy name is Noah. Oh, Noah," she exclaimed, "that's just wonderful! Listen, I'll do anything you think is necessary. If you want, I'll listen to you singing in the shower. Do you sing in the shower?" She giggled happily.

"I don't think you'll be questioned on my singing," he said, injecting a more sober note into the conversation, "but we have a lot of work to do in the next month and a half."

Still barely able to contain her glee, Maggie babbled on. "I'll sell Tupperware. I'll sell Avon. I'll volunteer for Girl Scouts Troop leader. What else can I do? I know—I'll make a snowman for the front of the house. Anybody who makes a snowman has to be a good person. Oh, and I'll buy a couple of bird feeders to hang from the trees and—"

"Whoa!" He laughed down at her. "Slow down. All you have to do is be yourself—Mrs. Noah Jamison."

Maggie raised her head and gave him a peculiar look that he couldn't quite decipher.

Noah bunched up his pillow and punched it. He pulled his blanket up to his chin and concentrated on falling asleep. He rolled over on his stomach and then on his side.

Opening his eyes, he looked at the shadows on the wall cast by the window blinds. There was no use fighting it. He wasn't going to fall asleep for a while.

He couldn't stop thinking about her. How he ached to smooth her silken hair back from her face, to stroke her slim neck, to hold her sweet face between his hands. He would undress her slowly, pausing often to savor her feminine charms. And when he loved her, she would cry his name in a frenzy of ecstasy such as she had never known.

And when she trembled in his arms, he would tell her not to be afraid, that she was all right. But was he? Was he all right? The thought sobered him. He didn't know what he thought or felt anymore. All he knew was that he wanted her and that he spent more time thinking about her than was healthy.

Maggie's gaze fell on the sliding lock she had attached to her bedroom door just after moving in. Maybe it was creepy of her, and maybe it showed an essential distrust of men, but it would make her sleep easier. And it did.

Just now, though, Maggie wished she didn't have that lock. She closed her eyes. The door would open slowly, and as silently as a whisper he would come into her bed. His strong, firm hands would wander at will over her secret places. Her hands would pass lightly over his hard, corded neck, the sinewy muscles of his arms, his chest matted with tightly coiled hair, thighs sheathed in steel, lips full with passion and tenderness.

Maggie groaned. Reaching out, she flicked on a small lamp and picked up a paperback.

CHAPTER SIX

"Jack and I are so glad you moved into the neighborhood!" Ellen, a perky next-door neighbor, leaned her head against her husband's shoulder. "Up until you guys came, we were the only newlyweds around, and with everybody celebrating tenth and twelfth wedding anniversaries, we felt kind of out of it—you know what I mean?"

No, what do you mean? Maggie felt like saying. She merely smiled.

Jack nodded emphatically. "Those guys are down to two or three times a month—not like Ellen and me and"—he elbowed Noah—"you guys. When we're not at work, we rarely see the light of day!" He guffawed.

Noah jumped up. "Anybody want a drink?"

"Sure," Jack replied.

"Sure," Ellen replied.

Maggie stood. "How about some munchies?"

"Sure," they replied, this time in unison, and laughed heartily at their ability to read each other's mind.

Joining Noah in the kitchen where he was squeezing limes for margaritas, Maggie rolled her eyes. Noah's shoulders shook with suppressed laughter. As he salted the rims of the glasses, measured out the Triple Sec and tequila, and dropped in ice cubes,

Maggie glared. "Be nice, sweetheart," Noah whispered. "They're our neighbors."

Nodding, Maggie decided to make the best of the evening. She put some crackers and cheese on a tray, filled a bowl with nuts, and took a deep breath.

"What kind of work do you do?" she asked, returning to the living room. She placed the snacks on the coffee table in front of their guests.

Ellen answered for both of them. "Jack does law, and I do a little of this and a little of that." She was a tall, attractive woman with well-cut black hair and long red nails.

"What Ellen means," the obviously well-fed Jack cut in, "is that I make money and she shops." His ruddy face was wreathed in smiles as he gazed fondly at his wife.

Ellen's scarlet lips were poised in a full, little-girl pout as she eyed her husband flirtatiously. When she turned her attention back to Maggie, her tone was confiding. "We're trying to conceive. I don't see any reason to wait, do you?" She addressed the question to Maggie.

Maggie uttered a weak laugh. "Why, no. I suppose not. It's a personal decision, though. I couldn't say." Surreptitiously she wiped the thin line of perspiration that had appeared on her upper lip.

Oblivious of the discomfiture of her hostess, Ellen chattered on. "After all, I'm twenty-nine years old, and my biological time clock is ticking away. How old are you, Maggie?"

Before answering, Maggie glanced at Noah. He looked apoplectic. "I'm thirty-one."

"Thirty-one! My, oh, my. Well, you two had better get busy!"

Laughing uproariously, Jack patted his lap. "Sit

here, honey. She sure is a card, my girl." He winked at Maggie and Noah.

"A regular barrel of laughs," Maggie said, careful to keep her tone neutral. She took a bite of her favorite cheese Danish. It tasted like plastic. Noah was unusually quiet, she thought, which was odd in itself but especially strange since he had admonished her to be sociable.

With careless aplomb Ellen moved on to the next topic. She stuck her hand out in front of her. "Do you like my ring?"

Maggie glanced at the huge marquis-shaped diamond. "It's very pretty. Have some cheese, why don't you?"

"My baby"—Ellen nuzzled her husband's cheek—"has wonderful taste. That was my engagement ring, and he just gave me this." She opened the collar of her cashmere sweater to show an even larger diamond pendant. "For our first anniversary." She giggled. "I can't wait to see what he gives me when we have our first child."

Maggie thought she was going to be sick. Surreptitiously she smelled the cheese to see if maybe it was spoiled. It smelled exactly the way you would expect Havarti to smell—creamy and mellow. Catching her eye, Noah gave her a broad wink. Her stomach began to settle down.

"Wouldn't it be super if we had our babies at the same time?" Ellen went on, totally unmindful of the fact that Maggie had said nothing about pregnancy or babies or about anything except cheese. "We could baby-sit for each other and have someone to talk to while walking the carriages around the neighborhood. Why don't we plan on it? Huh? Great idea? If we all try now, there shouldn't be more than a couple of months' difference. What do you say?"

There was a stunned silence. Maggie's mouth felt as if it were full of sand. She said nothing, for she knew the only sound that could come out would be a croak. Even Noah, famous at the newspaper for his quick wit, was at a loss for words. Ellen's lips glistened as, caught up in her daydreams, she wore a beatific smile. Jack emptied his glass, flicked his tongue around its rim, reminding Maggie of a jackal at a salt lick, and laughed giddily. "Honey"—he squeezed his wife to him and let his hand hang over her shoulder, perilously close to her breast—"I think you're jumping the gun a little bit. These people might not even want children." He addressed Noah. "My wife tends to get carried away. I hope she didn't embarrass you."

"N-n-no, n-not at all," Maggie assured him, her eyes riveted on his stubby fingers, which seemed to creep lower and lower by the second.

"Anybody for a refill?" Noah broke in.

"Why, sure." Jack held out his glass and nudged his wife's arm with his shoulder. "How 'bout it, honey?" Nodding, she put her head back, which had the effect of bringing her breasts another inch closer to her husband's dickering digits (Maggie looked away) and chugalugged the remainder of her drink.

"Maggie?" Noah looked at her. She shook her head. "Why don't you come on back in the kitchen with me and help squeeze those limes. I have a little cut on my finger, and that juice stings worse than old-fashioned iodine."

Grateful for the opportunity of escaping, Maggie hurried after Noah. Letting the door swing shut behind her, she bolstered herself against the adjacent wall. "Noah!" she wailed.

"Just think of it as a business meeting," he said,

trying to soothe her. "They're not so bad, anyway. They mean well."

"Oh, sure," she griped. "They mean so well, they'd probably talk about their sex life with the pope." Indignation welled up inside of her. "How could they talk about those things with people they just met? For all they know I can't have children for very real medical reasons. For all they know you're a—a— what do they call those people who have both male and female sex organs?"

"Hermaphrodites," he supplied.

"Yeah, for all they know you're a hermaphrodite!"

"Hey!" Noah protested smilingly. Cradling her face with warm hands on cool cheeks, Noah repeated, "Hey. Don't let it get to you. We know what we're doing and what we have to do to get what we want."

"Well, after we get the first baby, I promise you I will never walk a baby carriage around the block with *Her!*"

Noah smiled down at her. "If we need neighborhood references for the second baby, you'll walk to Timbuktu with her."

Maggie shivered, not so much because of his words but because of the tone of command he used with her. "Give me the limes."

"I'll do it," he said. "You just sit down and rest."

"What about the cut on your finger?"

"It was just a way of rescuing you. I wanted to give you some fortification before returning to that den of iniquity." He chuckled and pushed her down onto the nearest chair. As he did so, his lips brushed against the top of her head. "Your hair smells like wild flowers."

"It's the shampoo," she offered.

"No, it's your hair. Mm." He let his lips trail from

86

her fragrant blond curls to her earlobe to her throat and then, with widened eyes, she watched his lips approach her own. She was seized by panic. She leaned back, back, back, so far in the cane kitchen chair that in an instant the dizzying sensation of falling was upon her as the flimsy chair tipped over.

"Oops!" He hurled himself to his knees, catching the chair as her head was just a fraction of an inch from the quarry stone floor.

"Thank you," she gasped. She squirmed sideways out of the chair and onto the floor. Noah was still kneeling with the chair back in his hands. His mouth was twisted with pain. "What's the matter? Are you hurt?"

"Nothing much. I just wrenched my back. I'll be all right in a minute." The grayish tinge his complexion had assumed was replaced by a pale green.

"Should I call a doctor? I'm so sorry. This is all my fault." She wrung her hands.

"I'll be all right. If you want to be helpful, though, why don't you take this chair out of my hands and stand it up someplace where I can't see it?"

She hurried over. "Oh, of course. I didn't even think of it. I'm so sorry. You should have let me fall."

"Then you would have had a head like Humpty Dumpty's." His mouth twisted into a smile, and he let himself down on all fours as she relieved him of the chair. "I'll just stay like this for a minute and then I'll be all right. My back goes out every so often. It's nothing to worry about."

"What's going on in here?" Jack's voice boomed as he bounded through the swinging door. He stopped dead in his tracks. "Well, I'll be . . . Hey, honey, come on in here. You've got to see this. These guys are practicing some tricks from the Kama Sutra, it looks like. All our talk in there did ya some good.

Heh, heh, heh. One thing, though." Jack's brow creased into puzzled furrows. "I don't exactly get this position. How does it work?"

Maggie's lips quivered as she tried to hold in her laughter. Noah's face became mottled with rage, a far healthier color than the gray-green it had been. His voice was almost a snarl. "I twisted my back. That's all there is to it."

"I can help with that," Ellen piped up. "I'm a practicing chiropractor."

"Yeah, that's one of the 'little of this and little of that' activities she was talking about earlier," Jack put in with not a little pride.

Rolling up the sleeves of her clingy cashmere sweater, Ellen straddled a helpless Noah. "Now, this is going to hurt, honey, but the pain'll just last a second."

"You sure you know what you're doing?" Noah couldn't quite conceal the tremor in his voice.

"You're not going to break anything, are you?" Maggie asked with mounting concern. "Are you licensed? I don't know if I believe in chiropractic. What if you pull when you're supposed to push? What if"—her voice rose shrilly—"you do irreversible damage?"

All heads were turned in her direction, Noah's included.

"Give this girl a drink," Ellen ordered her husband. Dutifully Jack poured a stiff margarita using the lime juice that had remained in the juicer from the first round. Maggie shook her head. "Drink up," Ellen ordered, all vestiges of flirtatiousness gone.

Putting the drink to her mouth, Maggie puckered her lips. There was definitely something missing in this drink. As she swished the sour, salty mixture around in her mouth, she watched in horror as Ellen

88

gave what looked like a karate chop between the shoulder blades to Noah. The chop was followed by a series of sharp twists, pulls, and wringings. When she was finished, she stood up, rubbed her hands together, and held out her arm to Noah for support.

"That's okay. I'll get up on my own."

As he rose on one knee Maggie half-expected him to fall back prostrate and lie there till the ambulance and stretcher arrived. A little shaky, he nonetheless managed to stand on his own two feet unaided. Shrugging his shoulders clockwise and then counter-clockwise, he smiled broadly. "I owe you my thanks, Ellen. Where did you learn to do that?"

Ellen tilted her head to the side and smiled modestly. "The question is, how did you ever manage to fall like that?" She looked expectantly from Maggie to Noah.

"It was just one of those things," Noah said.

"Well, listen, you guys. I think we'd better pass on that second round tonight, don't you, honey?" Jack looked toward his wife.

"Absolutely." Ellen nodded emphatically. "We'll take up where we left off some other night. Next time, you come to our place."

When she had ushered her guests out the front door and said her final good nights and nice-to-know-yous, Maggie heaved a sigh of relief. Hurrying back to the living room, she saw that Noah was stretching his arms up over his head in order to get the last kinks out of his muscles.

"How do you feel?"

"I've felt better and I've felt worse. Injury in the line of duty. I get a purple heart for this one."

Remembering that she was dodging what was going to be a kiss, Maggie bristled. "I would hardly call that in the line of duty." Avoiding his eyes, she went around the room emptying the ashtrays their guests had filled and collecting empty glasses and crumpled napkins.

"They didn't turn out to be so bad after all, did they?" he called out to her as she was placing the glasses in the sink to be washed.

Maggie was formulating an answer in her mind just as the door bell rang. "Saved by the bell," she called out, and went to answer it.

There stood Ellen, a smile on her lips, and in her hands a package wrapped in white tissue paper stenciled with red arrows and hearts. "Here." She gave the package to Maggie. "I thought you might find some use for this." She giggled. "Especially tonight. It will really make him feel better. Believe me. I don't know if it will make him feel *that* much better considering what he did to himself, but it will hasten his recovery. If you use it right, he won't be out of commission for more than one night." She winked. "It'll be tough, but you can stand one night without him. Now all you have to do is put a liberal amount on the palm of your hand and rub deeply. Really dig in with your thumbs."

"Thanks, uh, but what is it?"

"Oh!" She laughed. "Didn't you know? It's erotic massage lotion. Ginseng. And you know about ginseng, don't you?"

Maggie shook her head.

"Ginseng," Ellen pronounced with an air of importance, "is an aphrodisiac. It's been used in the Orient for thousands of years and"—she giggled again—"I don't believe they're suffering from underpopulation in that part of the world!"

Maggie held the package out to Ellen, "Thanks, Ellen, but really, I don't think we need—"

"Nonsense!" Ellen said, dismissing Maggie with a

90

brisk wave of the hand. "It will make Noah's back feel better. If it has any other side effects, so much the better." She winked again and turned to go. "Enjoy yourselves!" Her voice rang out in the frigid night air.

Holding the package in her hands, Maggie closed and locked the door. When she saw Noah, he was laughing into his sleeve.

"What's so funny?"

"Funny? Funny? I don't see any banana peels around here for slipping on. Nothing at all is funny. Should I take off my shirt?"

"Noah! Giving massages is not part of the job description."

"Well, neither is acquiring a wrenched back!" He rose, she noticed, a little unsteadily.

"Here. Let me help you." She rushed over to the sofa and offered her arm. He took it gratefully. She felt a twinge of shame. "Massage, anyone?"

"That's an offer I can't refuse." He hobbled over to the dining room table. "Here?"

She hesitated. "Maybe your bedroom floor would be better. That way I can sit on your fanny"—she paused—"if I have to. That room has the plushest carpeting in the house."

"Seems like you've got it all figured out." His eyes twinkled.

Flustered, Maggie blurted out, "Don't get any ideas. This is strictly medical!"

"Of course."

As she followed him into his bedroom her mind reeled. This was to be the first time she would actually step foot in his room; she had always hurried past it, sometimes glancing inside.

His room looked cozier from the inside than it did from the hallway. There wasn't much furniture other than the open sofa bed, the type of solid oak secretary that had hidden drawers and compartments, and a rare Turkish area rug that he had thrown over the deep pile of his camel-colored carpeting. He stretched out on his stomach on top of the rug.

Maggie took a deep breath and flexed her fingers several times. "Don't you think you ought to remove your shirt?" She would have sworn she saw him blush.

"Of course. What am I thinking of?" He laughed and pulled himself to a sitting position.

Her eyes were on his chest as with the unbuttoning of the top two buttons, curly black hair spilled out over the white fabric of his shirt. As his shirt flapped open she had a crazy urge to slide her hands over the hirsute skin of his chest, to nuzzle against the prickly curls, kissing and nibbling. And when she'd have had her fill of such pursuit, she would slide her hands over the smooth, taut muscles of his shoulders in order to help him totally divest himself of the garment.

He lay his shirt down beside him, and crossing his arms under his forehead, he lay prostrate, ready for her ministrations. He squeezed his eyes shut tight, feeling the beads of perspiration standing out on his head. It wasn't the pain. He could endure pain. What he didn't know was whether he could endure Maggie's touch upon his flesh and know that he couldn't touch her in return. His nerves were aquiver as she lay first one tentative hand upon his shoulder blades and then the other. He clenched his teeth, wondering why he had ever allowed things to progress this far. He could have gone to his regular masseur at the club. Why did he always have to prove himself? When would he learn that he wasn't a man of steel?

Maggie chewed on her bottom lip as she unscrewed the cap of the ginseng massage oil. She sincerely hoped that it would not live up to Ellen's claims. From the way Noah looked at her from time to time, she tended to doubt that he needed an aphrodisiac.

The oil made a warm and fragrant pool in the palm of her hand. Very carefully, from her position at Noah's side, she let it drip onto his broad back. At first she just used the tips of her fingers to smooth it over every inch of skin. Then, with the heel of her palm and the ball of her fingers, she dug into the tight sinew of his back and the bulging muscles of his shoulders.

He groaned.

"Am I hurting you?"

"No, that feels good. Mmm." He lapsed into silence. Then, "A little lower is where I pulled it."

"Here?"

"To the right a little more. Up. There, that's it. Dig in as hard as you can. Ah, that's nice."

Sweat trickled down her nose. She had never realized what hard work it was to give a massage. Hard work, yes, said one small part of her brain. Delightful, sexy work, said another.

"You have a beautiful body," Maggie murmured.

He turned his head to the side and looked at her with one open eye. "Beautiful?"

"Beautiful." Feeling that she had said too much, she surrendered herself to the task at hand and concentrated on the area that was especially sore. However, she was so small and he was so large, it was difficult for her to reach over to that spot. When she changed sides, she found that the angle was incorrect, causing her own back to ache. With a sinking feeling she became aware that the only effective position from which to rub his lower back was sitting astride his rear end.

It was as if he had read her mind. "Why don't you get on top of me? You'll be more comfortable."

"Okay." The bottle of oil held tightly as if it were a life preserver, she hiked up her skirt with her free hand in order to straddle him. His buttocks were small and shaped like half moons. They felt firm against her inner thighs. She wished she had worn slacks tonight. The fine nylon of her panty hose provided embarrassingly little protection against the rough texture of his wool pants.

She poured more oil onto her hands and, using all her strength, proceeded to rub as deeply as she could. Her own shoulders began to ache with the effort, but she couldn't stop, not even for a moment, for then her position atop him would cease to be therapeutic and begin to be compromising. She concentrated on the knotted musculature, which hardly gave at all beneath her ministrations. She concentrated on the bone and skin, on the muscle and sinew, on—God help her—the smooth, rocking rhythm of her thighs against his hips as she worked his flesh. She heard not only the pulsating sound of her hands on his shiny, oiled skin, but also the erotic swish of nylon-encased legs with each ever-so-slight movement. The exotic, sweet scent of ginseng mixed with the clean male scent of sweat and something else, maybe desire. Her tongue flicked out over her lip, catching a salty drop of perspiration.

He groaned again. "Oh, yes. Yes. That's the way."

She redoubled her efforts, pummeling and kneading for all she was worth. Her blouse began to stick to her. Her hair was matted to the back of her neck. Her arms were beginning to lose sensation. She paused and looked at him. His back glistened in the light of the moon and his nightstand lamp. He reminded her in his male physical perfection of a Renaissance sculpture. He would have made a lovely model.

"That's enough," he announced suddenly. "I've been selfish. You must be exhausted."

"Well," she said, and laughed nervously. "I have felt fresher." Gingerly she lifted one shapely leg over him and rose to her knees. She screwed on the bottle cap and held the half-full bottle of oil to the light. "I guess this stuff works like magic."

"Uh-huh." He shook his head as he rolled to a sitting position. *This* stuff"—he pointed at her—"works like magic. And one good turn deserves another."

Maggie didn't respond right away. She was looking at his chest, at the way the black hairs fanned out and then disappeared into a thin line under his belt. She was looking at his midriff and thinking that even while he sat Indian-style there was not an ounce of extra flesh to be seen. He was in supreme physical condition. She shook her head quickly as if doing a double take. "What did you say?"

"I said, it's your turn now. I'm going to give you a massage."

"I don't need one."

"That's where you're wrong. You're going to be stiff in the morning if you don't let me at those overworked muscles. I have the feeling you're not used to such exertion."

"It's all right, really. I'll just take a hot bath."

"That you will." He smiled with what appeared to her to be genuine fondness. "But after your massage. Now, take off your blouse and lie down." He was all business.

"What are you talking about? I'm not taking off my shirt. Are you some kind of nut or something?"

"Maggie"—his voice was gentle—"I'm not going

95

to attack you. All I'm going to do is give you a massage, and I can't do it through your clothes. You'll feel a lot better. Believe me."

There was something to his voice, a softness, an authenticity, that made her believe him. And it was true that her arms were throbbing. And she had been fighting off a headache ever since that biological-time-clock talk. Maybe it wasn't such a bad idea. "All right, but you have to turn around."

"Agreed," he said with a chuckle. "Of course, I've never seen a bare-breasted lady before." She opened her mouth to protest. He held up his hands and backed off. "Not only won't I look, I'll leave the room until you're sure anything worth seeing is covered." She couldn't see his face, but she just knew he was grinning from ear to ear.

"You make me feel about as sophisticated as one of those contestants on TV game shows who scream and jump up and down every time they win a blender or an electric can opener."

Noah laughed. "Those contestants are cute. So are you." He walked outside the room and to the living room where he put Beethoven's Seventh Symphony on the stereo.

Meanwhile Maggie thought that having said she felt foolish did nothing to alleviate the feeling. She felt gawky and silly as she removed her blouse and took Noah's place on the floor. She settled down on her stomach, her arms securely at her sides. "You can come in now."

His footsteps resounded as he approached—a neat trick, she thought, considering the wall-to-wall carpeting and the violins crashing loudly from the speakers he had wired to the bedroom. It must be her imagination. She felt his presence as he knelt beside her.

"Your arms have to go under your forehead. You can't keep them like that."

"I'm comfortable like this."

"Fold your arms under your head so that your forehead is resting on your hands. The angle won't be right otherwise, and I'd probably pound your face into the floor."

Her arms felt as if they were glued to her ribs. It was with great effort that she slid them up under her head, not even lifting them off the ground. If her head was not to be mashed into the floor, it was another story with her breasts. She flattened herself as deeply as possible against the pile so that the most he could see if he were looking was the white undersides of her breasts.

Before starting what he assured her would be a semiprofessional Swedish massage, Noah pressed the tips of his fingers against her temples. "Close your eyes. Empty your mind." He rubbed the hollows on either side of the nape of her neck. "Now I know what they mean when they say, 'She had a swanlike neck.'"

"And I know what they mean when they say, 'She was a birdbrain.' What am I doing here? What? What?" She punched jestingly at the floor.

"Shh," he said, trying to soothe her. "Be quiet and enjoy the sybaritic delights you are about to experience."

"Huh?" She quirked one eyebrow at his fanciful flight of speech.

He laughed. She closed her eyes and concentrated on the sweet strains of music.

Rubbing the oil between the palms of his hands to bring it to body temperature, Noah saturated her skin with the thick, viscous liquid. Its heavy, redolent bouquet filled her nostrils to an even greater extent than when she had been doing the rubbing. As his hands started their inexorable travels over her back, her sides, her neck, her shoulders, it seemed that the center of her being was controlled by his touch.

She felt small under his hands. When he caressed her (fondled? no, massaged! how confused she was), it seemed as if her whole body would mold into his hands. She felt as though she fit into his grip, as though they were sized just right for each other.

Goose bumps rose on her arms at the thought, or at his touch. Or maybe it was the music. She wasn't sure of anything anymore. And then he was stroking her arms with brisk up-and-down motions.

With his thumb and forefinger he kneaded her neck. "You're fighting me. Try to loosen up."

"You call this fighting?" she joked feebly. "You should see me when I'm angry!"

"Your muscles are tight. You're tense. You needed this massage more than I did." Without warning her he moved down to her calves. "I hope you don't mind a little oil on your stockings. My hands are greasy." She felt her legs quiver under the assault of his strong hands. "Your calf muscles are tied in knots. Maybe that's why you've got beautiful legs. Your muscles are in a constant state of flex. Now just relax. Relax. Don't fight me, girl." He stroked and pressed her resistant flesh. "I think you need one of these massages every day. We ought to make it part of our daily routine. Why don't you just slip out of these?" He removed her shoes. Holding her foot up in the air with one hand, he stroked the arch with the other. Doing the same with the second foot, he openly admired it. "You have a high arch. That's rather elegant."

"So when did you become an expert on arches?"

"I'm an expert on all aspects of the female anatomy. Here, let me back at your shoulders. If you want to get a good night's sleep tonight, that's where we ought to concentrate." He moved back to her upper torso. Sliding one hand under her arm, he placed the other on her shoulder blade. "This is a technique of deep Swedish massage."

"Uh-huh." All she could think about was the rise and fall of the violins and of the hand that he had placed under her arm. It was perilously close to her breast. And when his hand brushed against it, she was not totally surprised, nor was the sensation totally unpleasant. In fact, she felt her nipple harden in response. A blush rose to her cheeks, and she pushed down harder against the rug. But for the curse of maddeningly responsive nipples!

"How does this feel?" He pressed two fingers deep into a nerve.

"Ouch!"

"Concentrate on relaxing and it won't hurt. Go with the pain." He made concentric circles around the tender area. His hand was still underneath her, pressing against her armpit. Her nipples, overly sensitive, were still too aware of his proximity. Suddenly he was on a different track. With both hands he started at her neck and slowly descended the length of her back to the swell of her buttocks. The sensation was exquisite, and she felt it in places he hadn't touched. His hands made her think of steel sheathed in silk. She choked back a cry. The music rose to a crescendo, drowning out thought and sound and reality beyond itself.

Later, when she thought about it, she didn't know why she chose to leave at that moment. Gathering her blouse against her front, she stammered a thank-you and fled for the safety of her bedroom. She didn't look at him, had no idea what he was thinking as she ran from the room. She left him watching the slowly spreading stain of ginseng oil on the carpeting, for in her haste she had kicked over the bottle.

Later that evening, as Maggie soaked in a hot tub, she felt that no amount of soaking could wash away the imprint of his fingers upon her flesh. But did she want to wash it away? Didn't she, in some deep and elemental way, desire him? Of course, she did! she answered herself impatiently. But there were lots of things she wanted that weren't good for her. And she didn't do them. Later, after the babies came and she had her own life again, there would be plenty of time to go out and have fun.

She lifted her leg in the tub and soaped it with a natural sponge. He had said her legs were beautiful. As she remembered his words she remembered the feel of his hands on her flesh—the way he rubbed her with a barely concealed sensuality. She wondered what it would be like to make love with him. She shivered in the hot water.

Closing her eyes, she slid way down into the tub. These crazy thoughts she was having just wouldn't do. Better to think of the day's work or even the state of the economy than to think of Noah.

Luxuriating in the soothing water, she felt her eyelids become heavy. She smiled to herself. And then her mind, as if to spite her, returned to the subject she most wanted to avoid. Whatever she could say about him, about his motives or his ethics, Noah had good taste in music. She was a Beethoven lover herself. And he had good hands. Of great hands he had the best!

CHAPTER SEVEN

The sound of raucous laughter floated into her bedroom, awakening Maggie from a deep sleep. Groggily she opened one eye to look at her alarm clock. Ten o'clock. A morning person, she couldn't remember the last time she had slept this late. Never mind. She had been working till the wee hours every night this week, and she had nothing urgent to do on this Saturday, anyway. Turning over, she placed the pillow over her head and tried to fall back asleep.

Staccato bursts of laughter continued like shots from a cannon piercing her half-slumber. Yawning, Maggie wiped the sleep from her eyes and tried to focus. Who was that laughing? Men in her house? Were they friends of Noah's? They had better not be!

Maggie stretched and tried to hear what was being said in the next room, but she couldn't make out the words. As she tied an old terry-cloth bathrobe around her waist and shuffled out for her morning coffee, without which she would remain comatose for the remainder of the day, she just hoped that the voices belonged to the local police collecting for the Benevolent Association or someone like that. Neighbors such as Ellen and Jack, whom she had not seen since their visit two weeks ago, she would not be able to tolerate upon first awakening.

"Morning, honey," Noah called as he caught sight

of her trying to sneak past the living room and into the kitchen. "Come on in and meet some friends of mine."

"Good morning," she answered as she reluctantly approached the three men who stood staring at her.

"Honey, this is Ed, my oldest friend." He pointed to a skinny man with glasses, whose curly, light brown beard covered half his face. "And this is Mike." In contrast to Ed, Mike was blond, round-faced, and cherubic-looking with sparkling blue eyes and a ready smile.

"And this"—Noah placed his arm over her shoulder—"is my wife, Maggie."

Maggie's mouth felt like foam rubber. "Pleased to meet you." The words came out garbled.

"Why, you son of a gun!" Mike punched Noah good-naturedly on the arm. "You didn't tell us you got married! I can see why you'd want to keep her to yourself"—he ogled Maggie—"but this is carrying privacy too far. What did you two do, go and elope?"

Noah grinned down at Maggie. "I suppose you could call it that."

Ed smiled shyly. "Congratulations to you two. I'm sorry to have missed the nuptials, but I wish you all the best."

Coffee, coffee. The word kept spinning around in her head. If she drank a big strong mug of coffee, maybe she would come wide-awake and realize that this was the tail end of a bad dream. In real life Noah would not be introducing her to his friends as his wife. Not unless he was suffering from temporary insanity. Maggie hadn't told a soul about their "marriage," and she could hardly believe that Noah would so blatantly breach the terms of their agreement. And before her morning coffee, no less!

"What do you do, Maggie?" Ed asked, pulling his

mouth into a grin, which somehow made him look like a carved jack-o'-lantern. She had never seen a pumpkin with a beard, but as she looked up at him, she couldn't shake the image. "Keep the home fires burning, or do you have a real job?"

"It's real, I think," she said hoarsely.

As she was about to excuse herself, Ed continued conversationally, "I can't wait to introduce to you my better half. She's an artist—does poster art. Yep, she takes care of three kids and manages to turn out a poster a week. She's making a fortune. That little lady's an industry unto herself. She's got more talent packed in that little body of hers than I don't know what. God's gift is what's in her. You'll have to meet her soon."

"I can't wait." She hoped that didn't come out sounding the way she felt. Anyone who had a husband who bragged about God's gift at ten o'clock on a Saturday morning was someone she could do without knowing. "Excuse me. I just woke up and, uh, I'm going to get my breakfast now." She smiled at Ed and Mike. When she turned to Noah, she let the smile freeze on her lips.

"Wait just a minute, there," Ed insisted. Reaching into his inside pocket, he pulled out a checkbook, scrawled out a check, and handed it with a flourish to Maggie. "That's a little wedding present for you two lovebirds. You buy yourself something nice with it." He winked at Maggie.

Embarrassment washed over Maggie in wave after wave. She looked down at the piece of paper she held in her hands. It was a check for one hundred dollars. She held it out awkwardly. "No, really, I couldn't. It's very nice of you, but please, no, take it back." She knew she was babbling. She looked beseechingly at Noah. He smiled noncommittally.

103

"Now, now." Ed took the check, folded it in half, and stuck it in the pocket of Maggie's robe. "Never refuse money. That's the first lesson." His laughter resounded through the house like a giant's hiccups. "You go on now and eat your breakfast and think about what you're going to spend that on."

It was with great relief that she escaped from the threesome. As she passed the hallway mirror on her way into the kitchen, she glanced at herself. Her face was pasty, the wrinkles around her eyes prominent, and her hair stringy. If she didn't wake up until she had her coffee, her face didn't wake up until it had its Max Factor. Well, if he wanted his friends to think he had an ugly wife, that was his problem. Wife! Whatever was she thinking of? she berated herself.

She was just pouring her second cup when Noah appeared at the kitchen's entrance. "The guys left. They got the impression you didn't want to talk, so they told me to say good-bye for them. You could have been a little more cordial. They *are* my friends."

Maggie slammed down the coffeepot and left her half-full cup on the counter. She walked to the kitchen window where she stood with arms folded across her chest before slowly turning to face him. "Are you out of your cotton-pickin' mind? Since when do you bring people in here, real people, and introduce me as your wife? Are we living on the same planet? I mean, whatever got into you?"

"Maggie." His voice was like ice. "For better or for worse you are my wife, and you'd better start acting like it before this whole thing blows up in our faces."

"Bye, bye, Charlie." She turned back to the window.

She winced as he grasped her arm in a viselike grip. "What's that supposed to mean?"

She didn't look at him as she spat out her words. "It

means, let's put an end to this childish charade because it probably won't work, and even if it does, I'm beginning to suspect that the price is too high!"

He dropped her arm. "You should have thought of that before. I've got too much invested in this now, and you're going to see it through to the finish. Understand?"

She raised angry eyes to his. "What I understand is that you're changing the terms of our agreement. How could you bring your friends here? Nobody in my life even knows about this place or about you!" She took a breath. "Not even my mother knows! Why, for heaven's sakes, am I killing myself keeping two residences, running back and forth to pick up mail and put out trash that I lug over to my loft so it looks as if I'm living there? Did it ever occur to you that by bringing those guys over here you might be wrecking things for me? Did it ever occur to you that I might end up feeling quite the fool?" As an afterthought she added, "And how do you think I felt when Ed handed me that check? I'll tell you how I felt. Like a jerk or a kept woman or—or both! What am I going to do with this check, anyway?" Pulling it out of her pocket, she waved it in front of his nose.

"Give the money to a charity."

"Good idea. That's the first good idea you've had in a long time!" She felt herself getting more and more wound up.

Suddenly he was grabbing her in his arms, and his lips were pressing down upon hers—his tongue invading her mouth, his teeth clashing against hers as she fought him. With a sharp push against his mighty chest she extricated herself from the unwelcome embrace. Her breasts heaving, she looked at him uncomprehendingly.

Raking his hand through his thick black hair, Noah shook his head. "I'm sorry."

"Why did you do that? Why?" she whispered. Inexplicably tears filled the rims of her eyes. An uneasy calm settled over her.

"I don't know. Well"—he shifted from one foot to the other—"maybe I do know. Sometimes you get me so mad, Maggie, I don't know whether I want to kiss you or slap you."

"Make sure that in the future you don't do either!" she snapped. She bent to scrape at a gummy substance on the floor, blinking the tears away.

"I don't know how this happened." He sounded sad. "Things just seemed to have gotten out of control. They were going well, weren't they?"

Something in his voice touched her. "They were okay." A vision of his two friends flashed before her. "But that was before you took us out of the closet."

He smiled. "I don't think we can handle it otherwise. This isn't such a big town we're living in. Sooner or later it's bound to come out that we're married, and then how are we going to explain it? This way we can pretend it's a real marriage that didn't work out and get a real divorce. Since we didn't have a wedding, we can throw a divorce party. We'll throw a super bash—embossed invitations with insults, and we can even have custard pies to toss at each other."

"You're not very funny," she said, pouting.

"Come on, Maggie. It wasn't such a terrible thing I did."

"Yes, it was. Now everybody is going to find out. What will my poor parents say?—the last to know."

Noah sighed. "All right, I won't tell anyone else. You don't have to worry about those guys. They don't

106

even live here anymore. They just came in from Chicago on business."

"Really?" She brightened up. "Why didn't you tell me?"

"I was going to, but you flew off the handle right away. Actually they kind of popped in on me. I was hoping you would keep on sleeping. Anyway, I kind of liked introducing you as my wife."

"Why?" Her eyes flew open.

Noah shrugged and chuckled. "I guess it's an adult version of playing house. That's what we're doing, after all. We're playing house. I'm the daddy and you're the mommy."

"But where are the kids?" Her smile was melancholy. Without waiting for him to answer she broached the next subject. "In a way this really is a game, but we don't know the rules. Real wives have to act nice to their husband's friends. Fake ones don't. Fake ones don't have to do anything in fact."

Noah scanned the kitchen with last night's pots still soaking in the sink and the previous day's breakfast cereal cemented fast to the bowls. "Fake ones sure don't do the housework."

"Fake husbands sure don't bring home the bacon —except for themselves," she retorted acidly.

"Hey, no fair! How many times have I offered to pay a greater share of the expenses? But, no! Maggie Clay is too proud. You're so proud, I wouldn't be surprised if you came down with a case of scurvy from malnutrition!"

"I would manage quite well," she shot back, "if you would turn out the lights when you left a room and keep the thermostat at a reasonable setting. It feels like a sauna in this house."

"I'll take care of the utilities," he offered quickly.

"We'll keep splitting them."

107

"Maggie, please. I insist. You've proved your point. You're a proud, independent woman. You're my business partner. I'll make a deal with you. You clean up the kitchen in the morning, and I'll pay the utilities. It's not a bad trade."

She hesitated. Images of sirloin steaks floated around her mind. The thought of one more peanut butter sandwich made her feel as if she would break out in hives. "Well . . ."

"That's settled." Noah smiled. "Let's go out to dinner and celebrate. My treat."

"I think that's going too far," she said primly.

"Okay. Let's turn the thermostat up five more degrees. Come on, Maggie. Let's go out to dinner. As friends."

"You won't bring any of your other friends here without warning?" she asked.

"Scout's honor. We'll stick to mutual ones, like Ellen and Jack."

"You always have to stick it to me, don't you?" she teased.

Noah's eyes twinkled. "Seven o'clock at Hoolihan's." As he turned to go he pulled at the ends of her terry-cloth belt, tightening it. "You even look good first thing in the morning."

Maggie smiled and picked up her cup of cold coffee, unthinkingly taking a big swallow. Somehow she didn't mind at all.

Since her marriage, Maggie had avoided seeing her mother alone. When she saw her parents together or in larger family gatherings, it was easy to keep the conversation light. She couldn't remember when she had talked so much to her mother about muffins or hem lengths. On one or two occasions she caught her mother smiling benevolently at her fa-

108

ther. You see, I told you she would eventually become domesticated; she'll settle down now, the smile said.

This Saturday's shopping spree was therefore something she could not finagle her way out of without hurting her mother's feelings. Coming on the heels of the morning's confrontation with Noah and his friends, it promised to be a breeze—as long as all they did was shop. If they stopped for lunch and a heart-to-heart, Maggie knew she was sunk. Her mother had always known when her daughter had something to hide or when something was bothering her. Quickly calculating her bills, Maggie figured that there was no way she could really afford to buy anything. She was going to be reduced to returning all her purchases on Monday. Oh, she sighed, the things one did for love or lack of money!

Maggie gazed up at the skylight of downtown Minneapolis's Crystal Court. The cut glass shimmered in the winter sun. The light bounced off the crystal squares and became muted as it flooded the shopping area. Lush plants hung from the second and third tiers so that if you didn't know you were in an urban mall, you might think you had walked into the pages of a modern fairy tale.

Shoppers hurried past, intent on completing their errands or on using one of the skyways that connected most of the major buildings of downtown Minneapolis. The only drawback Maggie could ever think of about living here was the winter weather. Twenty below zero was not uncommon, but with the skywalks, the city's architects were doing all that was humanly possible to banish winter for its residents.

"Maggie, dear, I hope you weren't waiting long." Her mother swooped down on her. "I got stuck on a phone call with Mae, and you know how difficult it is to get her off."

"That's okay, Mom. I was enjoying the Court." Her mother hooked arms with Maggie and proceeded to regale her daughter with stories about the family. "I saw Sally the other day. My, she's getting big. If you ask me, she's using her pregnancy as an excuse to eat all day. But she always had a tendency toward chubbiness. Not like you, dear. I suppose when your time finally comes, you'll look quite elegant, even in your ninth month."

Maggie looked at her mother through narrowed eyes. Ever since she was a child, she had always, with one secret part of her mind, suspected her mother of being a witch. She always knew when Maggie was lying or hiding her peas under her napkin or playing sick to avoid an exam. She wondered now if her mother was fishing or if she was simply indulging in idle chatter. She also wondered how her mother would take to an adopted grandchild. As she gazed at her kindly, wrinkled cheeks, the momentary concern passed. If her mother loved her, as she undoubtedly did, Maggie knew she would love Maggie's child, biological or adopted.

"Let's go to that wonderful shoe store on the second floor. I always have room for another pair of shoes in my closet. Don't you, dear?"

Maggie looked down at her scuffed black pumps and agreed.

Her mother wound up buying two new pairs of shoes. Maggie, insisting that nothing was comfortable —this one pinched her toes, that one rubbed her heels, this one was too pointy, that one's heels were too low—emerged from the store empty-handed.

Next her mother steered her toward a boutique that boasted Fifth Avenue fashions and prices.

110

"Try this little number on, dear. It will look adorable on you." Her mother held up a gray flannel miniskirt with a long, perfectly tailored Italian blazer.

"I don't know, Mom," Maggie said. "It's not really my style."

"What are you talking about? It's fabulous. Now come on."

Reluctantly Maggie headed for a dressing room. The outfit was smashing, but so was the price. As Maggie pirouetted for her mother and a saleslady outside the dressing room, she tried not to admire her reflection in the mirror. "It's too short. I don't like minis."

"They're in style," her mother insisted.

"They're not my style," Maggie countered. Not when she was living from hand to mouth, she thought. Her poor mother would be aghast if she knew how frugal her daughter, who had grown up with bells and ribbons, lace and leather, had been forced to become.

"I have something a bit more conservative," the saleslady offered with an affected English accent. She brought a procession of dresses, suits, and pants, which Maggie dutifully tried on and adamantly rejected.

Shaking her head in dismay, Maggie's mother bought herself a silk scarf. "Just so the saleslady won't feel we've entirely wasted her time," she whispered to Maggie.

As they stepped out into the mall Maggie's mother suggested lunch at an Italian café. Maggie was about to agree when she spotted Ellen walking toward her with another neighbor whom Maggie had recently met. Her heart raced. Adrenaline flooded her system. "Come on back in the store, Mom," she urged. "I've changed my mind about that first outfit."

Her mother took a double take. "Why, Maggie, whatever has gotten into you? You seemed so sure in the store. I thought you hated it."

"Come on back," Maggie urged. She was breaking out in a sweat. One more second and she would be seen.

"I think we should look around a bit more. If you're not sold on something, you shouldn't buy it. Look, there's a very nice little boutique across the way."

"Please, Ma!"

"Oh, all right."

Ducking into the store, Maggie stood behind a rack of dresses as her mother waited to the side of the saleswoman who was currently engaged with another customer. Occasionally she would push a dress aside as if she were considering it or desultorily pick up a price tag, but for the most part, her eyes were glued to the plate-glass window through which she watched the steady approach of the two Brooklyn Park women. Ellen was laughing uproariously about something. The other woman was nodding toward the boutique where Maggie hid. Maggie bent to scratch her foot.

After an extended period of foot scratching, during which Maggie caught both her mother and the saleslady directing peculiar looks her way, she peeked through the clothes rack. Horrified, she broke into a cold sweat. Not ten feet away from her, Ellen and her friend were, God save her, admiring the window display. Maggie squeezed her eyes shut and prayed for them to move on.

"What are you doing down there?" Maggie's mother called.

"Nothing."

"Well, then, get up!" She turned to the saleswoman whose nose was wrinkled and whose lips were pursed. "My daughter changed her mind about the first outfit she tried on, the miniskirt and Italian blazer. We'll take them." With a nervous glance at Maggie, she explained, "She must be tired."

"My foot itches," Maggie explained.

"Her foot itches," her mother echoed, and smiled weakly.

Maggie took another quick peek through the clothes rack and felt that if she were twenty years older, she would be suffering from cardiac arrest. The jig was up. She was about to be exposed. Ellen was tugging on her friend's sleeve, trying to convince her to enter the store. The other woman was making reluctant faces and looking at her watch.

"Do you know those people?" Maggie's mother asked.

"What people?"

"Those women you're sneaking looks at. Maggie Clay, what's going on here?"

"Nothing, really. I think I have athlete's foot."

Her mother clapped her hand to her mouth. "All those shoes you tried on. We'd better hurry back and buy them all before someone catches it from you. Athlete's foot! I never dreamed a daughter of mine—"

"We don't have to buy the shoes, Mom. I'm not barefoot."

"Never mind." Addressing the saleswoman, she said, "I'll pay cash for that, if you'll wrap it up quickly. We're in a hurry."

"You're not paying for it, Mom. Here's my credit card." Digging through her purse, she brought up the piece of plastic, which she held out to her mother from her position on the floor.

Her mother's brow creased, and her lips began to quiver. "Are you sure it's only athlete's foot? You're not having emotional"—she seemed to gag on the word—"problems?"

Maggie laughed dismissively and surrendered herself once more to her imaginary itch. When she peered once again through the clothes, she felt like crying from relief. They were gone! She rose to her feet.

"Feeling better?" the haughty saleslady asked warily.

"Yes, thank you." She smiled at her mother. "Thanks for offering to buy me the outfit, but I'm a working girl now, Mom."

"Nonsense. It will give me pleasure." Her voice was clipped. When she used that tone, Maggie knew it was useless to argue. She wagged her finger at her daughter. "You see a doctor on Monday, though. Athlete's foot, my word! Now to the shoe store." At the shoe store Maggie's mother managed to find three of the half-dozen pairs of shoes her daughter had tried, paid for them, and now piled the bags with shoeboxes in Maggie's arms. "You can take these to a shoemaker, and he'll stretch them, put in heel cushions, and do what has to be done to make them comfortable. Shoppers do have a responsibility to each other, dear. Athlete's foot!" She sounded aghast.

"Mom, it's not a social disease."

As they headed for the restaurant Maggie looked up and down the mall. Ellen and company were nowhere to be seen.

Lunch was pleasant, once Maggie's mother was assured that yes, she would see a doctor, and no, she was neither going crazy nor trying to avoid creditors. The athlete's foot story didn't quite ring true, Maggie knew, but it had been on the spur of the moment,

114

and she had never been a very good liar. Anyway, to spare her mother's sensibilities she should have thought of something prettier—like bunions.

Laden with packages, Maggie thought as she headed for her car that she would have to avoid going out in public places for the next several months. She would shop through catalogues and visit only in people's homes. She could do without any more close encounters of this most embarrassing kind.

"Honestly, Noah, I thought I was going to faint. And I think my mother thought they were going to have to take me away in a straitjacket. That would have taken the cake if she had seen me. Ellen probably would have asked me if the massage oil worked and then proceeded to describe the properties of ginseng to my mother!"

Noah was laughing so hard, tears were streaming down his cheeks. "I can just see you there—scratching your toes!" He took a sip of his wine. "Oh, I wish I'd been there!"

"Believe me, it's better in the telling." Maggie buttered a roll. "Anyway, I wound up with a lot of shoes."

"And an outfit." He looked at her approvingly. "It's beautiful on you. The mannishness of the tailoring accentuates your femininity. It gives a guy the feeling that beneath that prim and proper exterior there lurks a wildcat."

Maggie smiled. "Should I say thank you?"

"That wouldn't be inappropriate."

Overcome by an inexplicable shyness, Maggie looked at her miniskirted lap. She lifted a forkful of delicate goose pâté to her mouth. The restaurant Noah had chosen was elegantly understated. It was located at the top of one of Minneapolis's skyscrap-

115

ers. Its walls consisted entirely of windows, and its decor was the city itself. In the starry, moonlit night the dozens of lakes in the Twin Cities twinkled like sapphires. The skyline of the city, although lovely, was but a backdrop to Minneapolis's natural wonders.

Maggie gazed out at the orange moon and the lakes. "The glaciers did their work well."

Noah smiled. "Maggie, after—how long is it now, four months?—we're having our first date."

The skin on the back of her neck prickled. "This is just a dinner between friends. You said!"

"Look at all the time we've wasted," he went on, as if he hadn't heard her.

"Noah!" She took another sip of wine. "How are things coming along with the adoption plans?"

"Very well. The doctor's papers are all in. The lawyer's affadavits are signed, sealed, and delivered. The process is in motion, shall we say. All we have to do now is wait—and knock the socks off that social worker who's coming for the home study."

"How did you manage to do it all so quickly?" Maggie was awestruck. "I had so much trouble when I was doing it on my own."

"Talent and efficiency."

"One thing I admire about you," Maggie said, laughing, "is your modesty."

"You know what I admire about you?" Noah asked.

"No, what?"

"Everything."

Maggie smiled at him, happier at that moment than she had been in a long time. She started to tell him of her hopes for the baby she would get soon, of her plans for the future. They talked about their pasts and laughed when they found out they had gone to the same junior high school and flunked the same math class with Mrs. Monahan, who hated children and hated math even more than she hated teaching.

They learned that they had both been skinny, awkward adolescents who surprised all who knew them by blossoming into attractive adults. They learned that they both loved walking on deserted beaches and eating hot chestnuts on cold winter days, that they loved romantic comedies and murder mysteries and that they disliked anything by people with hyphenated names.

They learned that they enjoyed being with each other more than with anyone else they knew.

Having met at the restaurant, they each had their own car. On the drive home Maggie glowed. When she arrived at the house, it was to find that Noah had already gotten there and was waiting for her in the driveway.

"Hi again!" She fairly brimmed with good cheer.

"Hi. I thought I'd walk you in like I would a regular date." He laughed.

She went along with the joke. "I'd invite you in for a cup of coffee, except it's your house." They laughed uproariously as if they had each uttered brilliant witticisms.

When the laughter died, there was silence. They walked to the front door. His key already poised in his hand, Noah unlocked the door. After their animated discussion and uproarious laughter, the quiet of their house was eerie. They stood woodenly in the hallway.

"Well, about that coffee . . ." Noah said.

"Maybe we'd better forget it," Maggie put in hastily. "Coffee keeps me up at night."

"Oh, right. Me too. Well, then, I guess it's good night."

She tilted her head upward, half-expecting him to

117

kiss her. She closed her eyes and sensed his hesitation. What she felt a moment later was his knuckles chucking her under the chin. She opened her eyes to see his retreating form hurrying toward his bedroom.

CHAPTER EIGHT

As Maggie finished dressing and looked with satisfaction at her business-suited image in the wardrobe mirror, she thought of how wonderful everything seemed to her now. Her life was full. She had gotten a promotion at work and now, rather than handling incoming ads, she was going out to businesses soliciting advertisements for the newspaper. Little Jennifer Martin, her protégée, had taken on her old job at Maggie's recommendation. Now Maggie was working harder, earning more, and juggling her two lives more successfully than she had at first.

Neither friends nor relatives, not even her landlord, suspected that she was not living in her loft. It was odd, but when she went there, the faulty skylight, creaky pipes, and exposed beams seemed to lose a bit of their charm. The shifting and groaning of the cargo elevator that took her to her artsy abode alarmed her, and the few empty wine bottles and bent beer cans that littered her street grated on her now as they never had before.

Why, she wondered, was she so happy in this rambling house in the suburbs? Her answer was disquieting.

It was Noah. It was the half-hour they spent together in the kitchen having breakfast, that provided a focus and foundation for her days. It was a time that insulated her against the petty annoyances and disruptions that might otherwise assume too great an importance in her life. The thought was disturbing.

The rich aroma of fresh-ground coffee brewing drew Maggie into the kitchen.

"Good morning," Noah greeted her as he handed her a mug of coffee.

"Good morning." She smiled her thanks. "You're up early today." She saw that her newspaper was folded next to her napkin. Noah had already set the table using placemats with pictures of floating bananas and oranges, slices of toast, and brown eggs.

"I've got a busy day today. I'm interviewing someone on the crime commission. It seems like scandal is about to sully our fair state. This is on the QT by the way." He poured pancake batter onto a skillet.

"And you're going to break it in your column?"

"You bet. That is, if I don't get my neck broken first."

Alarmed, Maggie knit her eyebrows together. "You'll be careful?"

"Sure. Don't worry." Expertly he flipped the pancakes into the air. Out of the corner of his eye he noticed her consternation. "I was exaggerating. This is the clean Midwest. We're civilized here. The worst that can happen is that someone might puncture my tires." He grinned and tossed two pancakes onto a plate, which he handed to her.

He sat opposite her, covered his pancakes with Vermont maple syrup, and opened his newspaper to the front page. Maggie opened hers to the ads in the middle.

"How's the job going?" he asked over the top of his paper.

Peering over the top of hers, she answered, "Pretty good. It was an unexpected promotion."

"You get what you deserve."

His words somehow sounded familiar. She was struck by an uncomfortable thought. "You didn't by any chance have anything to do with it, did you? You didn't pull any strings the way you've been doing with the adoptions?"

"Of course not." He rustled his paper impatiently. "I only pull strings that have to be pulled." He laughed. "What's the job like?"

"There's a lot more responsibility, naturally, and a lot more hustling. I get to talk to people I would never otherwise meet."

"That's good, isn't it?"

She nodded. "Usually. Yesterday, though, I was trying to sell space to a real creep. He said he'd buy a full page ad if I went out with him."

"Did you?"

"Do you want this pancake in your face?" she threatened good-naturedly.

"I thought maybe he was good-looking," he deadpanned.

"If I weren't hungry this morning . . . ! I told him I was married."

"You see? I'm good for something besides getting you your baby."

"I guess you are at that." She smiled broadly and then quickly buried her head in the newspaper.

With her new job Maggie's hours had changed. Where before Noah had left the house by the time Maggie emerged from her bedroom and often days had gone by without their running into each other, now they left for work at the same time and saw each other every morning at breakfast.

"I guess we'd better be going," Noah declared as he looked at the wall clock.

"I'll just put these dishes in the sink," Maggie said.

"Why don't you save them for tonight? It's getting late."

"I'd better get home before you then," Maggie said, teasingly reminding him of their utilities-for-housework bargain.

"Otherwise you take a shower with cold water tonight," Noah joshed.

Slipping on their overcoats, locking their attaché cases, and holding their partially read newspapers under their arms, Maggie and Noah walked together to their cars, parked side by side in the driveway.

"Have a nice day, dear," Noah called loudly.

"You, too, honey," Maggie sang out. She was not surprised when Noah strode over to land a smackingly loud kiss on her lips. She, too, had noticed Ellen and Jack saying good-bye in front of their house. Whenever Noah or Maggie spotted a neighbor in the street or at a window they were sure to make a production of their morning departures. They would try their darnedest to keep up appearances!

Maggie opened one eye. Who was that ringing the bell? And why didn't they go away? Why wasn't Noah answering? And what time was it, anyway? She tried to ignore the chimes, but they simply wouldn't quit.

Sighing over the warm dream, which she couldn't recapture, anyway, Maggie rolled over and swung her bare legs over the bed. She shivered. She always slept in the raw. She had started the habit as a small rebellion against the conventions of a middle-class upbringing when she had gotten her first apartment and had quickly become accustomed to it. Despite Noah's well-set thermostat, early Minnesota springs were cold, and for the seconds between throwing off her covers and throwing on her bathrobe, Maggie froze.

"Coming, coming," she grumbled.

Opening the door a crack, she was greeted by a blast of cold air and the harried face of her next-door neighbor, with whom she was barely acquainted. Throwing the door all the way open, Maggie saw that the woman held a squalling baby in one arm and her two-year-old daughter close against her with the other.

"Alisha fell out of her crib. I think she's broken her arm," she explained in a panicky voice. "I'm on my way to the emergency room. Can you watch Megan for me?"

"Of course, Louise. I'll be glad to. Go on and don't you worry about a thing here." Maggie reached out to the little two-year-old. "Hi, Megan. Come on in where it's warm."

Drawing the bewildered little girl into the house, Maggie attempted to make her feel at home. She gave her juice, made her breakfast, and played "where is Megan's nose, mouth, belly button" games until she was hoarse. She drew pictures for the child, played charades, peek-a-boo, and "this little piggy went to market." When they both collapsed in a heap on the kitchen floor with "ring around the roses," Megan couldn't stop her giggling.

"I think she likes you."

Startled, Maggie looked up to see Noah leaning against the door jamb, his arms folded across his chest and his ankles crossed. He looked as if he had been there for hours.

"Oh, hi. This is Megan, Louise Murray's little girl. Louise had to go to the hospital with the baby," she explained, pulling the belt of her robe tighter.

Megan sat wide-eyed on the floor next to Maggie,

staring up at Noah in much the same way that Maggie herself was doing. "Me Megan," she said in her little baby voice. "Dat Mag." She pointed to Maggie and waited for applause from Noah.

Noah obliged and bent to tickle the little girl's tummy. Megan fell backward in a fit of laughter, and deciding that she liked this big, grinning man, she proceeded to regale him with her antics. She showed Noah her eyes, nose, mouth, and belly button and went through the entire routine Maggie had done with her. "Shirt!" She pointed to her shirt and to Noah's. "Shoes!" She crawled over to pound the points of Noah's loafers with her tiny fists. "Blue!" Amidst giggles she pounced on Maggie's bathrobe. "Belt," she said proudly, and yanked hard at Maggie's belt. Before Maggie knew what was happening, the robe had flown wide-open, exposing her in all her splendor to Noah's voracious gaze.

Maggie gasped, pulling the fabric around her. She looked with dismay at Noah. His eyes had darkened and seemed to grow wider. The blood pounding in her head, Maggie jumped to her feet. "I hope you enjoyed the view," she said with embarrassment.

"I did, thank you."

The child skipped around the room chanting merrily, "Naked Mag, naked Mag!"

Hurrying to her bedroom, Maggie called over her shoulder, "Watch her for a minute, please."

"Sure. One good turn deserves another."

Maggie drew her lips into a tight line and balled her fists. She could just imagine the smirk on his face!

She got dressed quickly, pulling on a baggy pair of cords and her bulkiest sweater.

When she emerged from her room, Megan was continuing her chant, and Noah sported just the smirk she had imagined.

"I liked you better before," he drawled.

"That's enough, Noah. One would think you'd never laid eyes on a woman."

"As someone once said, my dear, 'none to thee can compare.'"

Maggie flushed. "Megan, would you like to watch *Sesame Street?* Come on, let's turn on the TV and say hi to Big Bird."

"Naked Mag, naked Mag, say hi to Big Bird!"

"Nice name she's got for you," Noah said with a drawl. "Do you mind if I use it too?"

"Aren't you late for work, Noah?" Maggie retorted as she absently turned the channels.

"I've got a little extra time today. Anyway, I haven't eaten yet. Come here, honey," he called to Megan. "Would you like Uncle Noah to sing you a song?"

"Song," the child said with a happy nod.

In a surprisingly melodious voice Noah proceeded to sing a whole medley of children's songs. Soon Megan was gazing at him rapturously, thumb in mouth, clearly in love. Maggie tried not to listen as she puttered around the kitchen fixing coffee, taking out boxes of cold cereal and raisins. She let the spoons clatter on the table, let the water run longer than was necessary, tried humming herself. To no avail. If she were two years old, that voice would make her fall in love also.

By the time Noah had finished his impromptu concert, it was getting late.

"What are you making?" he called.

"An anchovy-and-olive omelet," she said, fibbing.

"I'm on a diet," he answered. It was with evident relief that he saw the corn flakes and bran cereal awaiting him. With no time to sit down, he ate his cereal standing up at the kitchen table and took his coffee with him to the car. "Are you going to work today?" he asked.

"I'll make it in sooner or later. Louise probably won't be too long. Anyway"—she turned to Megan—"we'll have fun this morning, won't we, sweetie?"

Megan nodded, and Noah smiled approvingly. "I think you'll make a good mother. That's nice to know."

"What's it to you?" Her voice was sullen.

He winked at her. "I wouldn't want to help anyone who wasn't deserving."

"I'm helping you, too," she felt like shouting at his receding back. She kept quiet. As Noah opened his car door he turned to her and waved cheerily. She blew him a kiss for old Mrs. Kemper, who was walking her dog in their direction.

The following morning Maggie awakened without benefit of her alarm clock. Hoping to make up for the previous day's breakfast fiasco, she dressed with care. The suit she wore was a black-and-white tweed; the blouse was white with a ribbon down the front, which she tied in a big bow. She wore sensible black pumps and swept her hair away from her face. She looked, to her eyes, meticulously professional and scrupulously un-sexy.

To Noah, some thirty minutes later, she looked deliciously wanton. She reminded him of a starched and straight-backed librarian who became a dance hall goddess when, in her secret life, she took down her hair bun and removed her glasses.

Though they generally took turns, Maggie had set the table for the second day in a row and was in the process of preparing the food. The newspapers were waiting, the breakfast placemats were shining, and the bacon was sizzling. She placed two perfect, sunnyside-up eggs on Noah's plate and one on her own. The bacon was crunchy and the coffee delicious.

"My compliments to the chef," Noah remarked jovially.

"Thank you." Her voice was as crisp as the bacon. She shook out her newspaper and proceeded to block out Noah's face and most of her light. When he shook out his own paper, her nerves pulsated with the slight noise. When he rose to get more coffee, she lost her place in the column she was trying to read. When he said her name, she jumped.

"What?"

"The food is very good."

"You said that already."

He cleared his throat. "Sorry."

From the time he had first laid eyes upon her that morning, Noah had not been able to shake the vision of Maggie sitting there before him, naked. He had not been able to shake that image all the previous day, either. What a magnificent woman she was! What he would give to make love to her, to make her scream his name in ecstasy, to squirm and pant beneath him. He would do almost anything for that privilege. But there was one thing he could not do. He could not jeopardize the adoptions. He could not mix business with pleasure. There were too many risks, and he wanted a son too badly. He would have to wait before he would have her.

The crackling of the newspaper pages as she turned them exploded in his ears like firecrackers. His gaze lingered on her slim, pale fingers as she picked up her toast. Her hair shimmered in the morning sun, reminding him of golden corn ripening on a late summer's field. He wanted to talk with her on this frosty morning—to have an innocuous conversation about work or even the heating ducts—to indulge in light banter. He could find no words.

When they left for work that morning, it seemed to him that a convention of neighbors had gathered. There was Ellen but not Jack. He saw Louise Murray's husband and Mrs. Kemper and her dog again. But somehow, though by all rights and common sense they should kiss and wave, hug and tease, Noah and Maggie went their separate ways in their separate cars with only the barest of muttered good-byes.

Work that morning wasn't nearly as interesting as Maggie had come to expect. It was nothing more than work. In her office a little before lunch, Maggie mentally tallied up her situation. She had sold two small ads, had had three appointments cancelled or postponed, and had shared an excruciatingly painful breakfast with Noah. In fact, the ads and cancelled appointments paled in significance with the tension she could almost taste at breakfast. She knew he was attracted to her. She had seen it in his eyes when he looked at her. She felt it in her own eyes when she looked at him. But she would not falter. Actions often had unforeseen consequences.

To the rapping that sounded at her office door she answered an indifferent "Come in."

"Hello, dear wife."

"What are you doing here?" She pushed back her desk chair.

"I work in this building, remember? Let's go to lunch."

"Together?"

"That was the general idea."

"We'll be spotted."

"Oh, gosh!" He snapped his fingers. "I hope they don't get the FBI, the CIA, and the KGB after us.

Well, if they do, I've got my passport ready. I'll stuff you in my suitcase and take you with me to Brazil where we can eat lunch forevermore in guilt and Portuguese."

"I'm in no mood for this."

"Gee, I'm sorry, Ma. Next time I'll call for an appointment."

"Noah, will you stop!"

He motioned her to get up. "Come on down with me to the cafeteria."

"Cafeteria?"

"Yeah, you know—the place where you put tin forks on a faded orange tray and buy green ham sandwiches."

"Noah, everybody will see us."

"Maggie, the first amendment to the Constitution guarantees people the right to eat lunch."

She felt on the verge of tears. "Why won't you be serious?"

"I am serious. Against my better judgment I've allowed you to handle this your way, and it's all wrong. We can't keep this marriage in the closet. What happens if the agency sends someone around to the paper asking about us? I doubt they will, but we have to cover all fronts. We can't be married for one set of people, and casual business acquaintances for another."

"I can't tell people now. They'll think I'm crazy! And I certainly can't tell my family and close friends. They'd be devastated."

"You should have thought of that before." The stony set of his face made him seem removed and untouchable.

Maggie covered her face with her hands. What had she gotten herself into? There was no way around it. She had gone off half-cocked, it was a mess, and if they got their babies out of it, it would be nothing short of a miracle.

She felt his hand, gentle on her shoulder. "Don't worry. We'll work it out. Let's go now."

She got up wearily and followed him out of her office and down to the basement cafeteria.

"The ham is pink today," Noah remarked, lifting the top slice of bread off his sandwich. "I'll have to talk to the manager about that."

Maggie was beginning to relax as she opened the lid of her strawberry yogurt. "So is the yogurt. This place is picking up. You know, I think maybe you're right about not keeping our marriage such a secret. I think I'll tell my boss and my secretary about it. Neither knows my family, and I doubt if they'd ever meet. Yes, that's what I'll do. I'll tell them I wanted to keep it a secret because we both work here at the paper and I didn't want any nepotism talk or gossip or anything."

"I'm glad that's settled." Noah looked at her intently. "I knew you could be reasonable if I gave you a chance."

"Hey!" Maggie laughed.

She was scraping the bottom of the carton with her spoon when Noah spoke again. "I've got two things to tell you."

Maggie put down the spoon. "Give me the bad news first."

Noah's grin was lopsided. "I'm not sure which you'll consider bad and which good. So, first I'll tell you which I would consider bad if I were you." He grinned boyishly. "I'll be away in Duluth for about five days."

Maggie felt a sharp stab of pain in her chest. She didn't let on that the prospect of five Noah-less breakfasts was very bad news indeed. "Have fun."

130

"Aren't you even going to ask why I'm going?"

"Why are you going?" she obliged.

"It's all part of that crime investigation I'm doing. It's getting more and more involved."

"Dangerous?"

"Nah. Don't worry. It's strictly small potatoes compared to the scandals they have out East."

"Who said I was worried?"

"I could see it in your beautiful blues."

Maggie was spared the necessity of further response by the greetings of two journalists who stopped at their table with fully laden trays. Glad that there were no empty chairs nearby, Maggie endured several minutes of small talk while waiting to hear the rest of what Noah had to say.

When the reporters had moved on, Maggie smiled impishly. "So, what's the bad news?"

"You have to rake me over the coals, don't you?" Noah's chuckle belied the complaint in his words. "The other news is that I want you to come with me to the Founders' party next Saturday night."

Maggie didn't have to think. "I'm busy."

"Break your appointment."

"I can't."

"What's so important that you can't cancel when your husband asks—no, pleads, no insists—that you accompany him to a very important affair?"

"I have to wash my hair."

Scowling, Noah pushed his chair back loudly against the floor. "Let's not start again. It's important for you to go because there's a good chance that we'll run into some people from the adoption agency there. Social-worker types always go to this sort of thing, and I have it on good faith that our very own Mrs. Bloope will be there."

131

"She's doing our home study next week. Why do we also have to see her at a party?"

"So she knows we're regular people." Noah's voice was exaggeratedly patient.

"If that's what you have in mind, the less she sees of us, the better!"

"Enough of these cat-and-mouse games now!" he exclaimed sharply. "I can only take so much of it."

"Well, la dee dah."

Noah's scowl deepened. Maggie pursed her lips. Her eyes flashed defiantly. His breath coming out like a snort, Noah exhaled loudly. Maggie arched her eyebrows.

Maggie broke the silence. "I have agreed to tell certain people here at work that we're married. I have agreed to kiss you good-bye in front of our house every morning. I agreed—I ought to have my head examined—to go along with this harebrained marriage of yours. All I ever do is agree, after a little objection for form's sake, but I will not—repeat, will not—go to the Founders' party. No, *non* and *nein*. My friends, my parents' friends, or even my friends' parents may very well show up there, and I am not going to take that chance. Do you read me?"

"Loud and clear," was his poker-faced response. "You're putting the adoptions on the back burner."

"You're an impossible man, Noah Jamison. Impossible!" She stood up to leave. "Have a good trip!" she tossed over her shoulder.

"Don't forget to starch my shirts, dear." Noah's scowl had evaporated, and the grin that replaced it extended halfway around his head.

"I'll starch your underwear instead!" she hissed.

With Noah's departure Maggie had thought she would feel freer in the house, more relaxed. It was

132

odd. Having lived by herself for so long before Noah, having a roommate took some getting used to. Now she had to get accustomed to being without him. That seemed even harder. But being alone had its advantages. And she had better concentrate on those advantages because after they both got what they wanted, she would be alone again. And it would be for a lot longer than five days.

She turned down the thermostat from Noah's seventy to a more comfortable sixty-five degrees. On the first day of his departure she left the breakfast dishes go till evening, and on the second day she left them till the third evening.

Just as she was finally getting around to doing the dishes crusted with eggs and ringed with soured milk, the door bell rang. Filling the sink with dishwashing detergent and hot water for the dishes to soak in, she ran to the door. To her dismay she glimpsed Ellen's face through the peep hole. Maggie hoped she hadn't come bearing gifts.

"Hi, there! I noticed that Noah's car's been gone. I figured you needed the company."

"How sweet of you to drop by," Maggie managed to say.

"So where is he?" Ellen's curiosity was clearly in a state of high arousal.

"Oh, Noah's on a business trip. How's Jack?"

"We're fine. We were saying the other day that we haven't seen much of you two lately. Jack and Noah have been playing racquetball, but you swish in and out of your house like a ghost. How about next Saturday night? You guys could come over to our house. We have some neat video games and some super movies for the VCR. I mean, like super, if you know what I mean. Like they're not even X-rated. They're triple-X. How about it?"

133

Maggie gulped and wondered if this was what was meant by swinging in suburbia. "Thanks, but there's a party that we have to go to Saturday. Anyway"— she gulped again—"we'd rather just chat when we get together. We can see movies any old time."

It was eleven o'clock at night when Maggie finally managed to usher Ellen out of the door. She entered the kitchen. The dishes, in their pool of sudsy water, seemed to blink at her. "Tomorrow is another day," she said aloud, and proceeded to bed.

On that other day, as with the preceding three, Maggie was forced to face a very unpleasant fact of her life. She missed Noah. Her mornings seemed empty without him. There was no reason to make herself look as beautiful as possible at an hour when the sun had not yet fully risen. There was no reason to drag herself out of bed for a long breakfast.

Mail from the adoption agency was piling up in his absence. Suddenly the agency was inundating them with notices and letters of intent and instructions. She tore open the envelopes as soon as she got them out of the mailbox. With Noah away she felt a little bit as if she were invading his privacy, even though the letters were all addressed to Mr. and Mrs. Jamison. Judging from the mail, things were going according to the master plan. Most of their records had been processed, their personal finances and letters of recommendation scrutinized, and their motives adjudged pure. The final hurdle was the visit from the social worker.

On the morning before Noah was supposed to return, Maggie sat at the breakfast table. She had turned on the radio loud and was listening to a disc jockey who, in the interests of entertainment, was insulting the owners of his radio station. It was strange, she thought glumly, how often people communicated by means of insults. A little bit like her and Noah.

When the phone rang, she made a dash for it, picking it up on the first ring.

"You were expecting my call, huh?" Noah said by way of greeting her.

"Noah!" Maggie's face was beet-red. "How are you?"

"Still kicking. How's the house? Any infestation yet?"

"What may I ask are you referring to?"

His voice was filled with laughter. "I'll bet you a hundred bucks you haven't cleaned a dish since I left."

Looking guiltily at the sink with the gray, brackish water and the dishes sticking up like icebergs, Maggie retorted weakly, "I don't gamble. And what about your car? It isn't exactly what I would call clean!"

"Ah hah! I was right! And to think what I have to tell you!"

"What is it?"

"I'm going to be staying here an extra two days."

She was dismayed. "You are?"

"You miss me that much, huh? Well, this story is hot. Things are breaking fast. Oh, by the way, I won't be able to make it home to the Founders' thing. I thought you might be relieved to hear that. So, you holding the fort down okay?"

"Sure, except that the water heater broke, the tub overflowed, the roof sprang a leak, and I've invited a colony of ants to make this their permanent address."

"I knew everything would be fine. Any mail?"

Maggie filled him in on the adoption news, told him about the invitation from Ellen, and finally stressed caution on his part. "No story is worth risking your life for."

"It's not serious. Believe me. You don't have to worry." His voice took on an oddly cheery note. "I'm glad to know you are, though."

After the connection had been broken Maggie stood against the wall, holding the buzzing phone. It was almost as if, she thought, she didn't want to let him go.

CHAPTER NINE

"It's so hard to get hold of you, dear. I call all the time and you're never home. I wouldn't have dropped in like this, except I thought your phone was out of order and you might be ill. Are you okay? How is your athlete's foot?"

The sight of her mother, touched-up blond hair perfectly coiffed, standing at the doorway to her loft at eleven o'clock Saturday morning put Maggie off-balance. Maggie was just on her way out, having made her daily trip to pick up the mail and check things out. "Oh, my athlete's foot. It's fine. A little Ben-Gay was all it needed."

Her mother pounced on the remark as conclusive proof of her daughter's terminal zaniness. "Ben-Gay's not for athlete's foot. Are you feeling all right, Maggie?"

"Fine. I haven't been home much. That's why you couldn't get me."

"Aren't you going to invite me in, dear?" Her mother stood on tiptoe in order to see what or whom Maggie was hiding.

"Of course." In her confusion Maggie had forgotten to let her mother enter. She swung the door open and stood aside. Her mother, trailing the scents of hair spray and French perfume, sailed past. She was a small woman, two inches shorter than Maggie, though her erect carriage and air of self-confidence made her appear taller.

"This place is stuffy. Don't you ever open any windows?" With two fingers she gingerly pushed open the streaked windows, careful not to let the grime come off on her. "I'll send over a window washer next week. It's a gift." She stilled the objections she knew were coming. "I saw Sally the other day. My, she looks robust."

Maggie grinned tightly. She'd known it would be only a matter of time before her mother brought up the subject of her pregnant cousin. She used to wait a few civilized minutes. Now she lost no time.

"It's such a wonderful experience for a woman." Her mother waxed sentimental. "To feel another life growing inside of you. Ah, well," she said, sighing. "So, Maggie, how's work?"

"Very good. I've been getting a lot of new accounts. It's very challenging."

"I never thought you'd grow up to be a career woman. A career is nice for a woman, but . . ."

"How's Dad?"

"Oh, your father is fine. He's a little restless since he retired. He needs something to do." She lowered her voice confidentially. "Now, if he had a grandchild to spoil, he would be a new man. You should see the way he looks at my sister and her husband. He's green."

"Should I make some tea, Mom?"

"Tea would be nice." Her mother walked around the loft, pausing to write Maggie's name in dust on top of the mahogany dropleaf table. "Maybe I should come in and clean one day."

Maggie bit her lip and tried to control her temper. "Sugar and lemon?"

"Just a little milk."

Maggie grimaced. There was no milk in the house. "Sorry, Mom. I'm out of milk."

"No milk in the house? You were always such a milk drinker. I guess you have no need . . ." Her voice trailed off.

Maggie's mouth grew dry. She poured some more water in the kettle for herself and tried to talk herself out of the burgeoning anger she felt toward her mother. She knew the woman wanted her to get married and have children, but she had never been so blatant and insensitive about it before. This had all started with Sally's pregnancy. She could just imagine how her Aunt Mae rubbed it in. She told herself that she must try to be understanding.

Her mother plopped into Maggie's vinyl recliner. "Are you seeing anyone special?"

"You don't waste any time with the amenities, do you, Mom?"

"What do you mean, dear?"

"I'm talking about all these questions you're asking."

"I only want what's best for you." Her mother lapsed into a hurt silence.

Guilt settled with a hard thump in the pit of Maggie's stomach. This was her *mother*. And if Maggie couldn't live her life according to maternal expectations, at least she could be honest with her. She poured the two cups of tea, handed one to her mother, and sat on the canvas sling-chair opposite her.

If she couldn't trust her mother, who could she trust? She mulled over her thoughts. She took a sip of hot tea, a deep breath, and plunged in. "Mom, maybe you'd better put down your tea before I tell you this."

Under her pancake makeup her mother's face went pale. She set down the cup.

"You are going to be a grandmother."

Her mother's face drained of its remaining color. She sat perfectly still, like a waxen figure.

"Mom?"

"Did you say what I think you said?" her mother croaked.

Maggie laughed nervously. "Yes, but it's not what you think it means. I'm not pregnant. I'm adopting."

"Oh! Oh! What a scare you gave me!" She laughed with relief. "Well, now, that's nice of you. You're taking in a foster child. There are so many of these children who need a nice person to live with for a while. How long will it be, six months or so?"

"No, you don't understand. It's not a foster child. I'm adopting a baby. You see," she went on in a rush, "I've wanted to be a mother for quite some time now, and I didn't think I should have a baby of my own, so I thought I'd adopt."

Arms akimbo, her mother sank deep into the chair. She put a hand over the right side of her chest. "My heart. I think I'm having a coronary."

Used to these histrionics, Maggie rolled her eyes heavenward. "Your heart's on the other side, Mom. Look, what's so bad about it? I think it's a great idea."

"A great idea, she thinks," her mother mimicked. "I'll tell you what's a great idea—for you to give up all this talk."

"It's too late for that. The papers are all processed."

Her mother got up as if to go. "Maggie, I have nothing more to say to you. It's your life. Your father and I tried to bring you up right. We failed."

"Mom, wait a minute."

"Where's my purse?" Her mother looked around absently.

"Here." Maggie held up the purse, which was in

plain view on the end table. Suddenly, more than anything in the world, she wanted to make her mother understand. She wanted her blessings and her goodwill. "Why won't you try to understand?"

"What's there to understand? My daughter's gone crazy, that's all I have to understand. Wait till my sister hears this. I'll never be able to show my face again. I just don't know anymore. You live your life right. You try to be a good person. You pay your taxes on time and you tip the trash collectors at Christmas. And what do you get for your trouble?" She sighed wearily.

"I thought you'd be happy for me."

"Happy! You want me to be happy that you're about to ruin your life?"

"I'm not ruining my life. I'm adopting a child. That's going to add to my life." Maggie kept her voice soft but determined.

"And think of that poor baby," her mother continued relentlessly. "What do you know about raising children?"

Maggie felt the blood pounding in her ears. If this were anyone but her mother, she would kick them out. "I know how you raised me. All I have to do is remember that . . ." She paused, and, somewhat placated, her mother gave a little expectant smile. "And do the exact opposite!" Maggie finished.

Her mother gasped. "My word!"

Maggie put her hand over one side of her face and closed her eyes. Nobody could accuse her mother of making this easy for her. "I didn't mean that."

Her mother cleared her throat. "You always did have a fresh mouth. You got that from your father's side of the family." She sat with her hands folded in her lap.

141

Maggie looked at her pleadingly. "Mom, I'm excited, and I was hoping you would be too."

Her mother looked away. "Who's going to give you a baby, anyway? You're a single woman and you work all day."

If she had gone this far, Maggie decided, she might as well spill all the beans. "I'm not single anymore."

Her mother let herself fall back onto the chair. "You got married?" Her voice was hushed.

"Well, sort of."

"What do you mean, 'sort of'?" Her mother's pitch was rising. "You're either married or you're not."

"All right. I'm married, but it's only temporary."

"Stop right there," her mother declared. "I don't think I want to hear any more. First you tell me you're adopting a baby. Then you tell me you're sort of temporarily married. What are you going to tell me next? That you've joined a cult and you're about to shave your head and wear bells around your neck?"

"You don't understand, Ma."

"You're right. If there's one thing you've said today that's right, that's it. *I don't understand. Will you please tell me what's going on here!*"

As logically and patiently as possible Maggie traced the train of events from the beginning. She began with her maternal yearnings and ended with her feelings for Noah. They were feelings she hadn't really known existed until right that minute when she expressed them. He was a man she cared for and admired and respected. He was the kind of man, she told her mother, with whom, under different circumstances, she might have fallen in love.

"This Noah person sounds competent at least," her mother relented. "Is he good-looking?"

"I think so. He's big and olive-skinned with doelike

142

eyes. And he has this look that makes you want to melt."

"Are you two"—her mother's hand revolved rapidly in the air—"doing anything?"

Maggie laughed. "Really, Mom. No, we're not 'doing anything.' We just eat a lot of breakfasts together and pretend that we're a typical married couple."

Her mother shook her head. "It's a new world. All right, Maggie, if this is what you want, I can't stop you. But I still don't understand why you won't do it the regular way. Surely you can get a real husband. You're a bright, attractive girl."

Was this what was meant by a generation gap? Maggie wondered. "I don't want to 'get' a husband. You 'get' cars and you 'get' shoes. If I ever marry—for real—it will be to the person I can't live without. Mom, I guess I don't expect you to see it my way, but can't you try to give me your support? Just because I'm your daughter and you love me?"

Her mother sucked in her cheeks. "For this I sent you to college? Ach!" She shook her head mournfully. "What can I do? I'm not happy about it, but I see your mind's made up. Whatever you decide, Maggie, you're my flesh and blood—"

"That's not the only reason, is it?" Maggie broke in. "Because my daughter won't be my flesh and blood, but I'm going to love her every bit as much as you love me. I know it."

"Me and my big mouth," her mother said wearily. "I know you will, Maggie. I didn't mean it like that. Come here." She stood up and held out her arms. Choking back emotions that reminded her of when she was a little girl, Maggie went to her mother and hugged her. "Don't worry about your father. I'll talk to him."

143

Holding her mother at arm's length, Maggie smiled. "I knew you'd come through."

"Well, I'd better be going. I have a lot to think about." She nodded her head as if she were making a mental tally. "I have to tell the family, I have to look at nursery wallpaper, I have to plan a baby shower."

"There's plenty of time for that." Maggie smiled happily.

"Am I ever going to meet this Noah of yours?"

"He's not mine, but I'm sure he'd be delighted to meet you."

"But you said you only see him at breakfast. That's kind of early for me to get over there." Her mother seemed to reflect. "Maybe I'd better not meet him for a while. You're sure there's nothing between you? You have"—her mother cleared her throat—"your own bedroom?"

"I have my bedroom and he has his. Your daughter is not living in sin. Never fear." Maggie laughed as she ushered her mother out the door. On the way out, her hair tousled by nervous fingers and her lipstick mostly off, the older woman did not appear quite so impeccably groomed as she had on the way in. Maggie felt a burst of tenderness for her. "Thanks, Mom," she whispered.

Her mother nodded resignedly. "It could be worse. You could have told me you were going over Niagara Falls in a barrel."

Maggie smiled. She knew that her mother, always embarrassed by overt displays of affection, didn't mean what she said. It was just her way.

After her mother had gone Maggie sat alone in her loft for a while, staring out at the gray street. It hadn't been an easy visit, but she was glad she had confessed all. Now that her mother knew, she felt freer, as if she had been relieved of a burden. Some secrets were

144

better left unsaid, and some, like this one, were much better divulged. It had been too late for her mother to stop her or to have any noticeable effect on her plans. And she would have had to find out sooner or later. This way, at least some of the pressure was off. There was enough to do, what with the actual plans for the adoption and the arrangements for the babies' care. She didn't think she had enough energy for another encounter with neighbors in the shopping center, and she certainly had enough shoes!

Noah Jamison sat on the edge of his sagging hotel bed in downtown Duluth with his head in his hands. It was three o'clock in the morning. He looked out across the alley to the large lighted windows of an old office building. His hands shook from lack of sleep. It wasn't only that where the bed didn't sag it had lumps and that the blanket was of some artificial fabric, which reminded him of Velcro. It wasn't only that after collating notes and analyzing his findings, he had to take out half the stuffing of his pillow and replace it with the notes for safekeeping. It wasn't only that he disliked hotels and always made sure that he could find the fire exits with his eyes closed.

It was—how he hated to admit it to himself—that he missed Maggie Clay. Why he should miss her, a woman who rarely had a kind word to say to him, was a mystery. But he kept imagining the tinkle of her laughter, so sweet and fresh. Her hair, which often caught the morning sun from her chair across from the kitchen window, reminded him of spun gold. She was so small, so soft, so fair. He looked down at his large hands, the backs sprinkled with black hairs. They were opposite physical types. Sometimes he thought of her as a delicate, exotic flower. If he were a plant, he would probably be a big, thorny cactus.

145

But if Maggie was a china doll, physically that resemblance ended when she opened her mouth. Then she became a firebrand! He laughed aloud, lying back in the hotel bed. He shook his head.

If only he could undo what had happened earlier that evening. All right, it hadn't been his fault, not exactly. The girl at the bar had been the one to approach him, after all. And he was a normal man, not exactly immune to the advances of attractive young women. And this woman was attractive. Hers was a come-on that couldn't be beat. She had cooed over him and batted long eyelashes and laughed uproariously at the embarrassingly unfunny jokes he had cracked. When she had asked him to drive her home, he could hardly refuse. And when she had asked him up for a cup of coffee, he hadn't seen the harm in it. When she had disappeared into her bedroom for a few minutes and reappeared in something "a bit more comfortable," what was he supposed to do—run for his life? He was a normal man.

It was only at the end, when she had wanted to make love, that things started to unravel. It was then that he pictured Maggie's innocent face, that he imagined what she would say if she knew. He thought of what it would be like to make love to Maggie. The feelings would be different. Almost without realizing what he was doing, he got up and dressed hurriedly.

When he left the girl's place, he had been full of apologies, had told her she was pretty and nice and thanked her for the evening. She hadn't seemed to mind, but her eyes glinted hard in the dim light where before they had glowed softly.

Noah stared at the place in the ceiling where the plaster was stained and peeling. He couldn't get a handle on things. He hated to hurt others' feelings, but even more than that, he was torn with confusion. Why, oh, why was he thinking of Maggie when he could have been making love to a sexy and willing woman?

Expelling air through his teeth, Noah raised himself with an effort. He had to get home. It wouldn't hurt the investigation much if he left a day early, and he didn't think he could stand one more day in this town. He stuffed his belongings into his suitcase, left a couple of dollars for the maid, and awakened the hotel clerk to check out.

The nighttime ride home along the frozen Minnesota roads was enjoyable. He had to drive carefully, but other than the great semi-trailers that rumbled by him every now and then, he was alone on the road. He was alone with his thoughts. And his thoughts centered on Maggie. How he longed to see her! He would be walking through the door just in time for breakfast. He could just see the look on her face now—surprise, joy, which she would immediately try to hide. Wouldn't that be just like her? He was assailed by a moment of doubt. What if . . . what if she had someone there? He turned the wheel sharply, almost swerving off the road.

He had better switch on the radio, he decided. Keep his mind on more mundane things. That, however, was not to be his fate. A newscast came on that had to do with the criminal case he was investigating in Duluth. It seemed that the district attorney's office had gotten involved and had subpoenaed some records that Noah had been trying to get at himself. He made a wide U-turn in the road. So much for Maggie and breakfast. He had a friend in the DA's office who was not averse to being named as an anonymous source.

Noah's return trip to Duluth proved worthwhile.

He got the information he sought and more "anonymous" quotes than he would be able to use. It was already far into the evening when he had gotten his notes collated again and had satisfied himself that there was nothing more of interest for him there.

His bones felt clogged with what he termed "sleep juices." But he had been guzzling coffee all day, and the lassitude in his bones was counteracted by a hyped-up nervous system, which made him jumpy. Under the best of circumstances he couldn't sleep well in that hotel. Tonight would be certain disaster. Sleep or no sleep, there was nothing for him to do but start the drive home again.

The radio blasted rock songs, and Noah sang along with the oldies. His trip had been a success, but now he felt happier than he'd felt since he left. He was going home.

As he pulled into Dallas Road he craned his neck to see his house. It was there, but something was missing. His foot was heavy on the gas pedal as he sped up to his driveway. Slamming on the brakes, he jumped out of the car and stood there, feeling bewildered and foolish. Her car wasn't here. Where was she sleeping? He didn't want to think about it.

He could almost feel the nervous energy with which he was functioning, shooting out through his fingers and toes, leaving him exhausted and weak. Shuffling like an old man, he made it to his front door, fumbled with his keys, and let himself in.

He was greeted by an odd sight. Sitting smack in the middle of the living room with the draperies pulled tight and only a single candle for illumination was Maggie. She had a deck of cards spread out before her.

The unexpected sound of a key turning in the lock made Maggie start. Her heart was pounding as she awaited the appearance of the burglar or worse. "Noah!" She jumped up and ran to the welcome, though unshaven, apparition. Throwing her arms around him, she felt his sandpapery cheek graze hers. "What are you doing home? I thought you were coming tomorrow night!"

Deliberately skirting the issue, he nodded toward the candle and drawled, "I'm glad to know you've been keeping the home fires burning."

"I was playing solitaire," she explained, as if that were all the explanation necessary.

"I see."

"Well, you see," they started in unison, and then broke off laughing. "You first," he offered gallantly.

"No, it's not important. You first. How come you came home early?" Suddenly realizing that they were still in a state of semi-embrace, she extricated herself entirely from his arms. "I was expecting you tomorrow."

"I finished early," he answered curtly. He wasn't about to tell her the real reason he had driven through the dark night on a full tank of gas but only a half tank of adrenaline. She would get scared and back off. He couldn't blame her. "What are you doing playing séance or solitaire or whatever it is you're doing in the dark? And where is your car?"

"Oh." She laughed. "That's because of Ellen. You see," she launched into the story of Ellen's surprise visit there and of the invitation to watch X-rated home video movies that night. "So, you see, I told her we were going to the Founders' party. That's tonight, you know, and if you had come home a few hours earlier, guess where we would be now, despite all my adamant protestations?"

Noah grinned, his energy restored. "So I would have won, after all."

"You didn't have to put it quite like that," Maggie teased with a coquettish sweeping of her eyelashes—it reminded him momentarily of that incident in Duluth that he was most anxious to forget. "Well, anyway," Maggie said, continuing her rendition of the evening's events, "I hid my car in the parking lot behind the market so she'd think I wasn't home. Knowing her, if she thought you had to prolong your trip and I was spending Saturday night alone, she'd drag me to her house, anyway, to see those blasted movies. And"—she laughed giddily—"I don't know which would be worse—seeing them with you or seeing them without you!

"And that, too, accounts for the candle. I didn't want her to see any lights in the house. There's not much besides solitaire that you can do in the dark."

Noah tilted his head and chuckled. "How come you didn't sleep in the loft?"

Maggie let her mouth drop most unbecomingly. Making a fist, she knocked on top of her head. "Hello! Anybody home? To tell you the truth, Noah, I didn't even think of it. I guess I'm so used to sleeping here." She was glad of the dim light, for she knew she was blushing. "So! Tell me all about Duluth. Did you get everything you need for the exposé? Are you going to put Jack Anderson out of business?"

Noah looked at her admiringly. She was better than a shot of adrenaline. "I'm not putting anyone out of business, but I have plenty of good material here, and there'll be some changes because of it. I'll be busy writing it up tomorrow."

"Too bad!" Maggie snapped her fingers. "You won't have time to do a cleanliness inspection of the house!"

"Maggie . . ." He stepped closer to her. "Maggie." Reaching out tentatively, he stroked her cheek with one finger.

Her heart seemed to stop beating. With widened, luminous eyes she looked up at him. "Oh, Noah." Once again she fell into his arms, pressing her face against the hard muscles of his chest.

"I missed you, Maggie." He lifted her chin upward.

She stood on tiptoe and slid her arms around his neck. "Breakfasts just weren't the same," she whispered.

"Shh." His lips closed down on hers. His one-day growth of whiskers tickled her gently as his tongue parted her lips. He probed deeply in her mouth, tasting it, exploring it, almost as if he had never kissed a woman before. At first his tongue darted gently inside and then with a quickening frenzy. When she answered his kiss in kind with her own eager exploration, he welcomed her. As their mouths remained locked his thumb began to rub against one lower corner of her mouth in a gesture that was excruciatingly provocative in its very simplicity.

"Ah, Noah," she moaned, coming up for air.

His hand left her mouth to cup her breast, first one then the other. They fit his hand perfectly, and he noted with satisfaction that the small peaks were already turgid and pointy.

She arched her neck back, overcome by a sensation of utter abandon. It was this, this for which she had been waiting all along. As he rolled the nipple of one breast between his fingers and bent his mouth to the other, it was as if a thousand volts of electricity passed through her. She bit her bottom lip, overcome by desire and need. But then she felt herself stiffen and she pushed at his shoulder.

"What is it?" His eyes pierced into hers as she moved away.

151

"I . . . I don't know."

He looked troubled. "Don't you want me?" He drew his index finger along the creamy top of one breast.

"Yes. No. I don't know." Her voice was raspy and low.

"You don't know," he said mockingly, and with both hands caressed her.

She kept her eyes cast down since the full force of his arousal and his power unnerved her. She didn't know if she could control him, or her own desire. Taking a step backward, she shook her head.

"Listen, Maggie, I don't play these games. We're both adults, so let's stop it."

"It's not a game," she answered, trying to force her breathing back to normal.

He raked his hand through his hair. "Maggie," he implored.

"No, we can't." Her voice was a plea.

"And I can't go on like this—having you but not having you." He paused. "When I was away, I almost made love to another woman. You know why I didn't?" He stared at her intently. "Because of you. Because of that face of yours that wouldn't leave my mind, because of those big eyes and that hungering, needing expression of your mouth. Because I wanted only you, and no one else would do."

Maggie's face mirrored her indecision. If she didn't stop now, she would go over the edge. That might jeopardize everything she had planned for. This marriage was for the sake of adopting children. It was not a marriage of love. Sex would only complicate things, perhaps threaten to ruin everything. Besides, her heart might be in jeopardy too. She just couldn't chance it. But, oh, how she wanted him. How could she help it? When he touched her, nothing else mattered. It would be so easy. She didn't know if she had the strength to refuse him. But she knew she must. "Please, Noah."

He had been studying her, and while he did so, his own mind was working. He knew she was right. His conclusions were remarkably similar to hers. He let out a deep breath and forced himself to utter words that made no sense to him. "Do you want to make that a game of gin rummy instead of solitaire?"

Swallowing convulsively, Maggie nodded. "Wait a minute." Straightening her clothes and patting her hair, she gave a small smile. She left to go to the kitchen where she took out two sodas and filled a bowl with potato chips, which she placed in the center of the floor exactly between them.

CHAPTER TEN

Today was the day! It was not yet seven o'clock in the morning and already Maggie was outfitted in old jeans and a sweatshirt. A broom was slung, military-style, over her shoulder. She swept in corners she had never seen in her six months in the house. She swept out closets and knocked spiderwebs from their safe havens. On her hands and knees, she scrubbed woodwork and kitchen chair legs, refrigerator gratings and aluminum window frames. Her arms ached, and the ammonia and water she used made her knuckles turn raw. Still she worked, cleaning with a fervor she had never known.

"Ouch! This place smells like a hospital." Noah greeted her with a yawn as he ambled into the kitchen.

"Careful! The floor's wet."

"I just want to get my breakfast."

"You'll have to wait till it dries. Why don't you clean out the rain gutters meanwhile? They're probably stuffed with debris."

"Maybe I should go back to bed and make my entrance over again. For some reason it sounded like you told me to clean out the gutters."

"Noah! The social worker's coming today!"

He affected surprise. "We may not be speaking the

154

same language, but we're definitely using the same calendar."

Wiping her brow with the back of her arm, Maggie stood up. "So, what are you waiting for?"

"You mean if we have dirty gutters, they don't give us any babies? Yep, I suppose I can see the rationale. It starts with dirty gutters. Next thing you know the babies will be drinking spiked formula and growing up to watch TV game shows. You can't be too vigilant these days. Is there any rule about cleaning the gutters after breakfast, though, or would that make me a communist sympathizer?"

Maggie suppressed an urge to splash her bucket of dark gray ammonia water on his red flannel slippers. "There's no time for kidding. We have a lot of work to do."

"Hi-ho, hi-ho, it's off to work we go, la-da-da-da, hi-ho, hi-ho, hi-ho, hi-ho."

"Are you quite finished?" Maggie swallowed her irritation with difficulty.

"Is the floor quite dry?"

"Oh, all right. Come in and eat, but slide along on these rags"—she threw over two halves of a towel she had ripped that morning—"so you don't muddy the place."

With another rag Maggie scrubbed at the yellowed wallpaper. Noah pulled out a chair, sat down, and jumped right up. "Why didn't you tell me it was wet?" He brushed at the seat of his bathrobe.

"You didn't ask." She smiled up sweetly at him.

"Maggie, don't start. It's too early, and it's too important a day to get off on the wrong foot."

"I've been slaving over this house since before dawn." Her eyes were accusatory.

"Don't blame me for that. If you'd kept up with the

155

housework all along, you wouldn't have so much to do today."

Kneeling on the wet floor, Maggie put her hands on her hips and scowled. "That's a classic male chauvinist remark. Why don't you do the housework?"

"Remember the deal? I pay more than you do. You're working off your debt." His grin as he unfolded his newspaper, reminding her of the Cheshire cat. "Anyway, you didn't have to start so early. She's not coming until midafternoon. You've got plenty of time. Why don't you sit down and have a cup of coffee?"

She sat down reluctantly and poured herself a cup of overbrewed coffee. "With my new job I can afford to pay more toward the house. The deal's off. The rags are in the cabinet under the sink, and there's a new mop behind the door. You can start in on the bathrooms if you don't want to clean the gutters now."

"Give the lady a mop and she becomes a drill sergeant. Equality, phooey!" he said, joshing.

She acknowledged his teasing with the faintest of nods. "Noah, I'm scared. What if she finds out about us? What if she asks us questions we don't know the answers to?"

"It'll be a cinch!" He refolded Maggie's newspaper, which she'd left strewn over most of the table that morning. "As long as you memorize the names of the Great Lakes, the National Parks, and the presidents carved on Mount Rushmore, you'll be in fat city!" Even as he made fun of her, he regretted it. "Hey," he said in a softer tone, "we'll handle her, and we'll do it so well that she'll never suspect she was handled."

"You're sure?" Her forehead wrinkled anxiously.

"Positive," he answered with more conviction than he felt.

Once finished with his morning toast and jam, coffee and cream, newspaper and jokes, Noah was more amenable to Maggie's suggestions. He drew the line at the gutters but was obliging about doing some yard work and helping her with the vacuuming and bathrooms.

Whoever thinks housewives don't do hard, physical labor, Maggie thought, has not been a housewife. After five hours of nonstop cleaning her hair was stuck to the back of her neck and muscles she had not even known existed ached. The house, however, sparkled. She stretched her weary arms and put away the cleaning supplies.

She looked forward to the next three hours before Mrs. Bloope's arrival. She would fill the time with a nice, long, hot bath, a manicure, and some soothing music to recuperate by. That would still leave her and Noah an hour or so to rehearse.

Then the phone rang.

"Hello. Why, hello, Mrs. Bloope. How are you? . . . Your schedule has changed? . . . Oh, I see. You want to come at one o'clock instead of at three-thirty? Oh . . . oh, no, of course that's all right. No trouble at all. . . . Fine. We'll be looking forward to seeing you. . . . Bye." For a moment there was an uneasy silence in the house.

"Aaiiieeeeee!" Maggie let go with a bloodcurdling scream.

Noah ran in from the yard. "What happened? What's the matter? Are you hurt?"

"She just called! She's coming! She's on her way!"

"Who just called?"

"Mrs. Bloope! She'll be here in half an hour! What'll we do? Oh, no! We're finished! This is the end! Kiss

157

your dreams good-bye!" Her whole body was shaking. Tears glistened in her eyes.

"Are those real tears?"

"Noah!" she screamed. "Did you hear me? She's on her way! Here! Now! Look at me! I haven't even taken a shower yet. My hair's a mess. My nails are filthy. My clothes aren't ironed, and I don't have any coffee cake to give her!"

"Oh, no!" He slapped his hand to his forehead. "No coffee cake!"

"Noah," she half-cried, half-screamed. "Don't do this to me now. Please!"

Noah grabbed her by the shoulders. "Calm down. Get ready, and I'll get the cake."

"But you have to get ready too."

"It only takes me a minute to blow-dry my hair." He grinned and patted her on the behind. "Go on."

Maggie frowned at him over her shoulder but decided to let the pat go by unchallenged. There were more important things to worry about now.

She must have looked like a character in one of those old-fashioned clips where the action is speeded up. It couldn't have taken more than five minutes, all told, for her to shower and shampoo. Drying and styling her hair was another matter. There was no way she could rush that. As the minutes ticked by she realized that she would simply have to leave the inner layers of her hair damp. Rather than take the time to give herself a manicure, she clipped her nails short. She traded elegance for seriousness. What self-respecting social worker, she thought to herself, would be impressed with red nail polish, anyway? From her closet she pulled out a simple, mauve knit dress that never needed ironing.

As she was blotting her light pink lipstick the door bell rang. Her heart skipped ten beats. She felt like she was about to go hang-gliding off Mt. Everest! She felt like she had to go to the bathroom.

"How do you do, Mr. Jamison."

Maggie, holding onto the wall for support, peeked out into the living room. Noah had just opened the door for Mrs. Bloope and was blocking her from Maggie's view. Maggie could hear her, though, and her voice was silvery and thin, almost childlike.

Maggie ventured out to greet her. She hoped Mrs. Bloope wasn't a handshaker because her own palms felt as if they were still soaking in ammonia water. "Mrs. Bloope? How nice to meet you." Maggie smiled.

"Mrs. Jamison." Mrs. Bloope inclined her head and held out her hand.

Maggie swallowed and took the proffered hand. She tried to shake using only her fingers. She hoped Mrs. Bloope wasn't one of those people who judged others by their handshakes. She surely must have felt that she had been shaking hands with a mackerel. "Won't you come in?"

As they adjourned from the foyer into the living room, Mrs. Bloope moved her head from side to side. Maggie hoped that she hadn't forgotten to remove one of her neat little piles of dirt with the dustpan.

"Where would you like me to sit?" Mrs. Bloope asked. She was a large woman with bushy eyebrows and a thick, coppery braid coiled around her head.

Maggie indicated the sofa, which was undoubtedly the most comfortable place to sit. Mrs. Bloope arranged herself at one end. She leaned against the satin-soft sculpture shaped like a seashell, which doubled as a throw pillow. No, she didn't lean against it. She was crushing it. The soft scalloped edges were bent in half beneath her elbows.

Maggie sat on the other end of the couch, and

Noah seated himself opposite them in a Queen Anne chair. Maggie smiled at Mrs. Bloope. Noah smiled at Maggie and at Mrs. Bloope. Mrs. Bloope leafed through the pages of her notebook. Getting right down to business, she began, "I see you have an application in for two children."

"Yes, that's right," Noah agreed.

Maggie's smile grew so wide, her cheeks began to hurt.

"Why two?"

"A boy for him and a girl—" Maggie began nervously.

"We just like children," Noah said, heading her off. "The more the merrier." He laughed.

"Yes, that's right." Maggie realized her gaffe. "We adore children. And two doesn't seem much harder than one, and I'm sure it will be lots of fun and the children will enjoy having siblings."

Mrs. Bloope's nostrils flared. Maggie thought, with a sinking heart, that the social worker was angry at what she had said but then Mrs. Bloope sneezed. "Do you have a tissue?"

"Oh, yes, of course." Maggie jumped up to get a box of tissues. She ran into her bedroom, only to find the box empty. Noah's bedroom, as well as his bathroom, were likewise devoid of all tissue boxes. Running into the kitchen, Maggie threw open all the cabinets. There was plenty of canned soup, plenty of scouring powder, plenty of everything—but no tissues. She ran back into the bathroom and unrolled a large wad of toilet paper. Class, she thought, real class. "I'm sorry," she said with a nervous laugh, "we're out of tissues."

"When you have little ones," Mrs. Bloope said after blowing her nose, "you'll never be out of them." She

160

looked up suddenly. "I hope. Now, then. How long have you wanted children?"

"Oh, a long time," Maggie replied.

Noah nodded.

"And why have you chosen to go with a private agency rather than with the state?"

"Well, there's such a long waiting period with the state that we thought we'd be better off adopting privately."

"Then money is no object?"

"We have enough for the adoption procedures." Noah took over.

"I see." Mrs. Bloope's voice was neutral. Maggie thought that her 'I see' would have sounded the same had they just confessed to a mass murder. "Who is going to take care of the children?" She looked at Maggie.

"We both will," Maggie answered quickly. She had known this one was coming.

"You work, I see."

"Yes."

"You'll give up your job to stay home with the babies then?"

"Yes, she will," Noah replied.

"Not exactly," Maggie answered at the same time.

Mrs. Bloope's eyes darted from Noah to Maggie. "I'm sorry?"

"What she means—" Noah started to explain.

"Why don't you let Mrs. Jamison tell us what she means?" Mrs. Bloope suggested.

Maggie's impulse was to get up and go hide in bed. She resisted it. "Noah and I can arrange our schedules to complement each other. That way we can both work and both take care of the babies."

Mrs. Bloope nodded approvingly. "That's quite modern. Are you sure it can be done?"

"Oh, yes. Noah can work at home. He's a columnist, you see. And I sell advertising, so my time is flexible."

Mrs. Bloope nodded as she jotted notes. "Now, then, your letters of recommendation are in order. It seems you are both upstanding and sober citizens. You don't drink or gamble or indulge in any of the, ahem, vices. What are your bad habits?"

Maggie smiled and shrugged her shoulders.

"What she means, Mrs. Bloope, is that we don't have any bad habits."

"One that I can see, Mr. Jamison, is your habit of explaining your wife."

Noah's face turned a deep shade of pink. "Sorry," he muttered.

"Now, then." Mrs. Bloope flipped the pages of her notebook.

Maggie thought that if she heard one more 'now then,' she would run screaming from the house.

"What are your views on discipline?" For the next two and a half hours Mrs. Bloope put them through a rigorous interview. She asked their opinions on just about everything, no matter how obscure. Every now and then she would write furiously in her notebook. At those times Maggie could hardly breathe. She wondered if Mrs. Bloope knew everything, could read her mind, even knew about the time in first grade when Maggie had stolen an eraser from the girl sitting next to her.

As the interview wound to a close the questions became more innocuous. "Well, then. Do you like your neighbors here?"

"Some of them are nice." Maggie nodded as she spoke.

"They're great," Noah said, once again at the same time.

Mrs. Bloope pursed her lips.

"Some of them are great," Noah amended quickly, "and some are, uh, nice."

"Yes, that's right," Maggie agreed readily. "There's a wide variety of people in this neighborhood. Really. There are great ones and there are, uh, nice ones." She smiled brightly. "The little girl next door is two and she's just darling, and we have some very interesting neighbors across the way. And, oh, there are some wonderful dogs that live on this block."

Mrs. Bloope's lips remained pursed.

"Did you see our swing set out back, Mrs. Bloope?" Noah asked a little desperately.

"Why, no, but perhaps you could give me a tour of the house first. Of course"—she looked around—"you have adequate space here."

Maggie led the way. "This is the kitchen." She looked proudly at the hygienic kitchen. See how clean it is, she felt like saying. You could eat off the floor!

"What's that odor?" Mrs. Bloope's nose twitched. "It smells like chemicals."

"Oh, that!" Maggie uttered a light laugh. "That's from when I was cleaning this morning the way I do every day."

"Harrumph!" Mrs. Bloope frowned. "With babies in the house you'll have to be a bit more prudent in your use of cleansers. Old-fashioned soap and water is the safest."

"Yes, of course." Maggie's head bobbed up and down. "I like soap and water best myself."

"Me too," Noah chimed in. "There's nothing like soap and water."

Maggie was startled. She'd forgotten that Noah was trailing along behind them. Her eye caught the square white bakery box on top of the refrigerator.

"Oh, Mrs. Bloope, can I offer you some coffee and cake?"

"Well, then. I suppose you can." Mrs. Bloope smiled. "If you don't mind, I'll just go freshen up first. Which way to the powder room?"

Maggie pointed her in the right direction, turned to Noah, and pretended exaggeratedly to wipe her brow. "Thanks for going to the bakery," she whispered.

Noah smiled. "I got an assortment. I thought it was fancier than plain coffee cake."

Maggie opened the white box and put the contents —small cheese, cherry, and apple Danish pastries— on a cake plate. "It looks excellent."

"So do you. You are excellent. Come here, Mrs. Jamison." Pulling her toward him, he planted a tender kiss on her mouth. His lips were soft and pliant and warm. She felt gooseflesh prickling on her arms. She would have liked to savor that brief kiss. When he let her go, he brushed her breasts ever so lightly with his fingertips.

"Not now!" she gasped, feeling her nipples rise as if at his bidding. "I mean, no, not ever." She stood still. Mrs. Bloope was making her way back to the kitchen. Maggie wished her arousal weren't so terribly obvious. If only she could slow her quivering breath! What a time to be betrayed by her own body! Clenching her teeth, she glared furiously at Noah. His grin, she realized, could only be described as roguish and self-satisfied.

"Danish pastries!" Mrs. Bloope squealed. "My favorite!"

Noah's face glowed. "Let me do the honors." He poured coffee for Mrs. Bloope and Maggie. He poured a tall glass of milk for himself.

"Well, then. You don't bake, I see." Mrs. Bloope addressed the statement to Maggie.

She sat with shoulders hunched and elbows on the table. "No, but—"

"But she's planning on taking it up," Noah interjected.

"I see."

"Yes, he's right." Maggie smiled brightly. "Noah and I believe in home-baked goods."

Mrs. Bloope quirked one thick eyebrow. "I noticed on my way back to the kitchen that you have three bedrooms. I didn't think you'd mind. I just took a quick peek."

"Not at all." Maggie thought she was going to be sick. She searched frantically back in her mind to assure herself that no telltale signs of Noah's occupancy had been left in the third bedroom. She and Noah had taken some pains to move many of his things into the master bedroom, but in their haste today, something might have been overlooked.

"Do you have an overnight guest staying with you?"

"Uh . . ."

"We did," Noah said with a smile. "Would you like another Danish? Why don't you try the cheese this time?"

Mrs. Bloope helped herself to a cheese Danish. "The middle bedroom appears to be in use."

"Oh!" Maggie laughed. "We use it as a guest room and as an all-around catch-all, whoever-wants-to-use-it type room." Whatever that meant, she thought.

"I see. Delicious Danish."

"Mm. It is good." Maggie agreed and bit into her second Danish, though she had absolutely no appetite.

Noah's hands tapped on his knees as if they had a

165

life of their own. He drained his glass of milk and took a third Danish. "These sure do go fast. Not as fast as homemade, though," he hastened to add.

In his eyes Maggie caught a mute appeal. "If you're finished, Mrs. Bloope, perhaps you'd like a look at the yard. It's not too cold out today."

Mrs. Bloope brushed the crumbs from her lap. "I sense spring coming. It's a late one this year, but it can't get away from us entirely."

"No, it couldn't," Noah and Maggie agreed. "Spring will have to come eventually."

The big backyard boasted a complete jungle gym and swing set left by the owners. In addition there was a small fenced-in area presumably for a dog. There was a partially rusted grill on the redwood deck.

"Do you do much barbecuing, Mr. Jamison?"

"In the summer. Sure."

"Your grill is rusty." Mrs. Bloope's tone was accusatory.

"Yes, well, I believe in disposable grills. I buy a new one every year. Heh, heh."

"Waste not, want not."

"Now that's a fine proverb, Mrs. Bloope. It's one of my favorites. Would you like to take a stroll around the yard? The ground is still frozen, but I do appreciate the fresh air."

Seen from the yard, the house looked eminently respectable. "That house there needs children, Mrs. Bloope. It's crying out for jack-o'-lanterns on Halloween and the pitter-patter of little feet on Christmas morn," Noah said earnestly.

Maggie jerked her head in his direction. Pitter-patter of little feet? Was that Noah talking, or had an alien being taken control of his body? Of both their bodies? He must be worried about this interview.

166

Mrs. Bloope smiled noncommittally. "You two haven't been married long. Tell me again why you didn't try to go through the state rather than a private agency?"

"There's a long waiting list with the state," Noah replied. "And at our age . . ."

Maggie's lip curled. She looked down at her hands, expecting to see blue, gnarled veins. At our age indeed! "Oh, look!" She pointed to Mrs. Kemper's dog, who had just moseyed into their yard. "There's one of the dogs I was telling you about. Here, boy. Here boy!" Bending, she patted her knee. The dog wagged its tail but kept its distance. "This neighborhood's perfect for dogs and children."

"I'm a dog lover myself." Approval gleamed in Mrs. Bloope's eyes. "People who love animals usually make good parents."

Maggie heartily agreed, though she thought the logic rather queer. She tried to whistle through her teeth so she could pet Mrs. Kemper's dog. The dog, not used to being whistled at by Maggie, nervously bared his teeth and put his snout to the ground. "Such a cute dog," Maggie said. He circled around and around one of the bushes that lined the back of the house. Stopping finally at a spot which he dug at with his hind legs, he stared at them defiantly and leaned back on his haunches.

"Why, I daresay he's doing his business behind the bush!" Mrs. Bloope exclaimed.

Noah shrugged and smiled. "Dogs will be dogs."

Louise Murray, followed by little Megan, emerged from her own house into the adjacent backyard. Megan waved. "Hello, naked Mag," she called, and collapsed in two-year-old giggles. Louise pulled the child to her side and admonished her sternly.

Maggie waved at her and turned to Mrs. Bloope. "She's an adorable little girl."

"What was that she called you?"

"Oh, I don't know. She has a different name for me every time she sees me." Maggie lowered her voice conspiratorially. "The influence of television, probably."

Mrs. Bloope's head bobbed up and down. "I'm sure you're quite right about that. I don't think you'd be the kind of mother who would sit her child in front of the television set while she did the housework."

"Oh, no, never."

When they returned inside, the odor of ammonia hit Maggie in the face, making her eyes tear. She'd been used to it before, but coming in from the fresh air, it struck her that the house smelled unnaturally of disinfectant. She smiled feebly at Mrs. Bloope. "I think I will stick with soap and water in the future."

As Mrs. Bloope made ready for her departure, Noah offered to wrap up the remaining Danish pastries for her to take home. When she refused, he gulped and stuck his hands in his pockets, looking for all the world like a schoolboy. "How did we do, Mrs. Bloope?"

"Why, whatever do you mean?"

He swallowed again. "Do you think we'll make good parents? I mean, will you recommend us?"

Mrs. Bloope smiled. "My recommendation is confidential, I'm afraid. But I'll tell you this." She paused. Her small blue eyes twinkled merrily. "I think you're both adorable."

As she closed the door behind Mrs. Bloope, Maggie dragged her feet into the living room where she plopped on the sofa. Noah followed, close at her heels.

"We blew it," she said.

168

"No, we didn't. She liked us."

"Everything that could go wrong did," she said morosely.

"No, it didn't. Ellen and Jack could have come by and invited all three of us to a swinging suburban switchies party. By the way, you did some pretty fast thinking today."

"So did you. We believe in home-baked goods, huh?"

Noah chuckled. "And you clean the house every day and think dog messes on your property are cute, huh?"

Maggie drew her knees up to her chin. She laughed awkwardly. "And so on, ad nauseum. Do you want to go out and eat Chinese food?"

Noah nodded. "Let's order one of everything on the menu."

CHAPTER ELEVEN

Tiny Jason fell asleep in Maggie's arms. Wiping the milk from the corners of his lips, she placed the sleeping baby in his crib. She stood smiling over him for a long time, marveling at the tiny feet, the little hands curled into even littler fists, the delicate features. There was a tugging in her heart as she straightened up and turned to tiptoe out of the room.

Since their first meeting with Mrs. Bloope, things had moved quickly. She had come over to the house several times after that to observe Maggie and Noah together. Both Maggie and Noah relaxed considerably compared to that first never-to-be-forgotten meeting. Still keeping up their pretense of having a regular marriage, they nonetheless were as natural and as honest as possible with Mrs. Bloope.

In a little more than a month they got their first baby. It was a boy and as per the agreement, this one was for Noah. Also as per the agreement, Maggie shared in his care. This was the hard part. Every time she held the infant in her arms, she wanted to weep. He was so sweet that she had to steel herself against covering his tiny face with kisses. The more she tried to harden her heart, the more little Jason chipped away at her reserve.

Whenever he would burp, she interpreted it as a smile just for her. When he cooed, it sounded to her ears like a precocious baby-talk version of *mama*. When she pressed his velvety head against her breast to quiet him, she felt that she would never be able to let him go.

It was with great relief that she would leave for work and hand over her part-time charge to his daddy. Mrs. Bloope had been vague about the second child, unable to say when they could expect her. Of course, since they already had their visitations and papers, the time period should be considerably shortened. It was that hope that kept Maggie going during those first weeks after Jason arrived. The sooner she had her own baby and could get back to her own place and her own life, the better for all parties. Not only was she concerned about her feelings for Jason but also she equally feared that he would grow too fond of her.

If it was true that every cloud had a silver lining, then Maggie thought her particular lining was in the form of changed daily schedules. Things now were so rushed that she had less time than ever with Noah. Lately she had come to realize that she looked forward much too much to the breakfasts with him. But now, leisurely breakfast banter was a thing of the past. Now it was grab a cup of coffee and a slice of toast and off to work! Noah left early for the newspaper where he submitted the column he had written at home the previous day and where he gathered research materials for the next day's work.

When he, laden with books and papers, came through the front door, Maggie tore out. She made most of her appointments now for the afternoon or evening. Somehow, in between all the entering and exiting that was going on, one or the other of them managed to do the shopping and all the chores that were necessary when a baby ruled the roost.

Now Maggie let herself collapse on the living room sofa. She was in a perpetual state of exhaustion. Jason woke up every two to three hours throughout the night, and though he was technically Noah's, Maggie took turns with him on the night shift. If all went well, he would sleep for at least an hour or two more, giving her time for a much-needed shower.

Closing her eyes, Maggie let the water beat down upon her shoulders. The bathroom was steamy. The sound of the water pounded in her eardrums. She could have luxuriated in the delicious sensations for hours, yet a kernel of worry nagged at her. Though she'd left the bathroom door ajar so she might hear Jason if he awoke, she feared that the sounds of her shower might drown out his infant cries.

Maggie smiled. If she'd been asked before Jason's arrival if she believed that a child's every desire should be indulged, she would have stated a very adamant no, of course not. Now that she was in charge of the real flesh-and-blood Jason, however temporarily, she found that she flew to him at his slightest whimper.

How good the hot water felt on her weary muscles! With her eyes still closed she let her head fall back and lifted her face directly into the shower's spray.

She didn't hear him when he entered. Then she felt his hands encircling her waist. Involuntarily she quivered. He did not say a word. Slowly his hands slid up her rib cage. When he reached her chest, he stopped. Spreading his fingers, he dug the heels of his hands into the bones supporting her bosom. A moment's hesitation and his hands were closing over her breasts, cupping the delicate white flesh, allowing the rosy nipples to peek through the space between his fingers.

172

Maggie gasped as exquisite sensations coursed through her. She shivered, though the steamy room was warm. Her eyes remained closed, allowing her to shroud herself in a thin cloak of anonymity. They were not Noah and Maggie in the bathroom of their suburban house. They were two wanton strangers meeting by chance in a tropical rain forest.

"Maggie," he rasped, breaking the spell. Turning her around, he grabbed her, one arm around her shoulders, the other hand tilting her chin toward his face. "Open your eyes." His eyes bore into her. Mesmerized, she felt herself drowning in their brown-black depths.

When he kissed her, she felt that he tore away any last shred of resistance she might have harbored. Dimly, through the drugging intensity of his embrace, she realized that he was standing in the shower with her and that he was completely dressed. The sopping-wet cotton of his shirt felt heavy with the weight of the water. His shoes squeaked, and as she looked down, she saw that they both stood in muddy pools.

"You're dres—" she began as she came up for breath.

He stopped her in midsentence. With the tip of his tongue he traced the line of her lips. Pushing her back lightly with one hand, he, too, took a step away. He stared at her face and then lazily, almost insolently, his eyes blazed a path to her toes, stopping for a long while at her breasts, tarrying at the gentle swell of her stomach, trying to unlock her most intimate secrets. "How wise of God to hide with silken curls that which man is most interested in," he whispered lasciviously.

Maggie froze. Had he thought about it for days, he could have chosen no words to embarrass her more.

173

She fought a sudden urge to cover herself with her hands. He must have read her mind, for he grasped her two wrists with his hands and held them at her sides. He smiled at her, and then he placed a reverential kiss on each of her breasts.

"Come," he whispered. Stepping out of the shower, he held out a thick Turkish towel for her. Quickly divesting himself of his clothes, he let them lie in a sodden heap on the tile floor. "May I borrow your towel?" Reluctantly she relinquished it, once again leaving herself naked under his scrutiny. She regretted the intimacy that had passed between them.

"I'm sorry," she said haltingly. "I can't."

Sweeping her up in his arms, he carried her off to his bedroom. "Let me down." Her voice was weak. Her eyes fastened on the pearls of moisture that lay atop his chest hairs. Surely it wouldn't hurt to do it just this once.

"Of course," he rasped, a devilish grin tugging at the corners of his mouth. Pulling back the covers, he lay her on his bed. With nary a wasted moment he began to stroke her. Burying his head in the hollow between her breasts, he licked a sensuous line to her navel. "If you could know how long I've wanted to do this." As if to emphasize his words, he kissed her with renewed vigor.

With a muffled moan Maggie let herself go. She wrapped her arms around his neck, arched her back, and let her tongue dart inquisitively within and around the recesses of his mouth. Tentatively she stroked his cheek, shadowed with the beginnings of stubble.

"Oh, Maggie." He planted kisses on her hair, on her neck. He nibbled at her shoulder. "Have I ever told you what beautiful shoulders you have?" Laughing and embarrassed, she shook her head. "Oh, but you do," he insisted. "Round and soft and firm and feminine. And golden, like the rest of you." Taking first one breast in his mouth and then the other, he suckled her long and passionately, causing her ever-responsive nipples to harden into stiff points. She let her hands slide down over his narrow hips, over his muscular buttocks. Slipping out from under his grasp, she took a moment to look at him. Unclothed he was magnificent. From his sinewy neck to his well-developed chest, from his slim waist to his wonderfully muscled legs, he reminded her of a magnificent male animal. While she, herself, was a hungry kitten. Then she forced herself to stop thinking.

With slow, sensuous abandon she let her hands slide over his chest, reveling in the feel of its soft, springy covering. She let kisses drop like dew in the path of her hands. With her teeth she tugged teasingly at the black curls. She breathed in his musky male scent and thought that this was where she belonged and where she wanted to be.

The late-morning sun shone through the windows in shafts, highlighting first one part of the room or one part of an anatomy and then another. Maggie laughed when his buttocks, caught in a natural spotlight, glowed.

"Don't laugh at me, lady," he said with mock fierceness, and catching her hands, he lifted them behind her head. It was then that he first entered her. She gasped at the initial sweet sharpness and then relaxed for him. With his knees he pushed her legs farther apart, as far as they could go. His command was total, wrought with finesse and a surging power. His confidence was supreme, and he displayed it with each movement, with each withdrawal and each plunge, with each kiss. "Wrap your legs around me." She obeyed him immediately and unquestioningly.

Never had she felt this urge to give herself so totally to another; never had she needed to feel mastered. Yet with Noah she wanted to let him know that at that moment, a moment she wanted to remain frozen in time, she was his. What he desired was her wish; what he wanted of her she wanted of herself. She was expectant. As he made beautiful, rhythmic love to her she sensed that he could and would make her rise to yet unimagined heights.

He was big and dark. He was hairy and he was strong. To Maggie he was Man. Holding him tightly against her, she moved her thighs slowly and silkily against his hips. She matched her movements to his, tightening her muscles around his pulsating desire.

He groaned. "You're good, sweetheart. You're fantastic. That feels wonderful."

His words incited her to a feverish pitch of excitement. She wanted to be the best he'd ever had. She squeezed harder. "Do you like that?"

"Mmm," he responded. Using supreme control, he slowed his movements to a stop, then withdrew. "I want this to last, woman." Unwrapping her legs from behind him, he lay one leg straight down on the bed. The other leg he bent back at the knee and pushed up so that she felt, under his eager scrutiny, even more exposed than she ever had before. The length and breadth of his hand covered her completely, gently stroking, teasing, exploring her most intimate secrets.

It seemed natural being with him like this. She wondered if he could tell how completely she delivered herself to him. She wondered if he knew that she had never been with another man like this. No, never like this. A husky moan emanated from the back of her throat. When he entered her again, she welcomed the sensation of fullness and felt that somehow this intimate connection could now never be broken. She felt his weight, his sheer heft, as it gently crushed her breasts and hips.

Their movements acquired a pace of their own as their bodies took over. Maggie mindlessly reached up to him, arching her back to stay in contact with the source of her erotic joy. Their undulations continued as they thrashed about Noah's bed with its crisp cotton sheets and even as they rolled over one another in a dizzying topsy-turvy of mutual, long-denied hunger.

The tide of their lovemaking ebbed and flowed as their syncopated thrustings and archings transported them both to a plateau of pleasureful abandon. They'd reached the point of no return. There would be no slowing down, no more prolonging of the ultimate melding of two eager bodies. Noah lost himself to his passionate desire, and she met it with an equal ardor.

The sun moved behind the shadow of a storm cloud. It was then, with the room pitched in semi-darkness, that together their ultimate release came, exploding within them like the furious clashing of hot and cold, of rolling sea and thunderous sky. "Oh, oh, oh, oh, oh, Noah, Noah." She held on to him as if he were her only link to the world of material objects, as if he were her savior and her inquisitor. Her vulnerability struck him anew, and he kissed her with sweet tenderness.

They had scarcely finished when Noah picked his head off her shoulder. "What's that?"

"It's Jason." Maggie wriggled out from under Noah. Hesitating, she glanced at him. Giving a self-conscious little laugh, she pulled the top sheet from his bed and shyly wrapped it around herself.

He looked up at her with an amused grin. "There's one thing I don't understand. Don't the parents usually make love before the baby comes?"

Picking up a pillow that had fallen off the bed, Maggie threw it smack in his face and trailed off to the, by now, squalling baby.

At work later that afternoon, Maggie sold more advertising for the paper than she had done to date. It was as if, imbued with the glow of love's aftermath, she was invincible. To the frugal protestations of businessmen who didn't want to spend more money for advertising than had been budgeted, she countered with well-reasoned arguments, facts and figures to prove that they would come out ahead. "You can't make money without spending money," was her oft-repeated refrain.

She was on top of the world. Her euphoria knew no bounds. She had that very morning made exquisite love to her exquisite temporary husband. He had evoked feelings and responses in her that almost surprised her. All she knew was that she felt wonderful. The first bluejays of spring were peeping out from behind new buds. Things were going her way.

With spring in the air she decided to walk the mile or so to her next account. Passing a public phone booth, she was struck by an urge to speak to Mrs. Bloope and find out just where things stood with the baby girl she had been promised. She didn't know why she had that urge then. Maybe it was superstition. Maybe it was that things felt too good. She was too happy. She wanted to make sure her happiness was real.

"What!" she screeched into the phone, not caring

that passersby stopped to stare. "Don't tell me that! It's impossible! You said so yourself!" She listened for a minute. "I don't care what the situation is. You promised me a little girl, and no, I am not content with just one baby!" A sob tore from her throat. "I am not losing control of myself. Don't tell me to calm down! I am perfectly calm!" She listened to what Mrs. Bloope was saying. "How could they change policy after we've been promised the baby?" She wound the telephone wire tightly around her wrist. "Yes, Mrs. Bloope. I apologize for yelling at you, and of course I understand that there are other people who don't even have one child yet. But no, I don't think I'm being selfish in wanting two babies within a few months. We have gone through quite a lot to get the babies, Mrs. Bloope. You must understand what a terrible disappointment this is."

With great effort Maggie articulated her words clearly and controlled the pitch of her voice. "When will we be able to get her, Mrs. Bloope?" Maggie swallowed the lump in her throat. "Two to three years? Did you say two to three years?" Maggie supported herself against the graffiti-decorated white-plastic sides of the telephone booth: "JoJo loves Sue"; "For a good time call Katie at 427-8892." The graffiti blurred in front of her eyes. "Mrs. Bloope? Mrs. Bloope, isn't there anything you can do?" Maggie noticed a man looking impatiently at the telephone. She turned away. "Mrs. Bloope, is there another reason you won't give us a baby girl?" Paranoid fantasies were beginning to prey on Maggie's mind. Had Mrs. Bloope discovered what they had been hiding all these months? "I see. You know we're good parents, but the agency feels that it has a responsibility to other good people as well." She repeated the social worker's officious words. "But there are so many babies, Mrs. Bloope. There are so many babies in orphanages in so many different countries. Surely you can cut through the bureaucratic tangle!" There was a sour taste in her mouth and a sharp pain beneath her rib cage. "Yes. Of course I know you are doing your best. All right. I understand. Yes, I know. Goodbye, Mrs. Bloope."

Maggie cancelled the appointment she had to sell newspaper space. She cancelled the appointment after that one too. She just walked and walked. She didn't pay attention to where she was going. She didn't much care.

Her whole world was crumbling before her eyes. Mrs. Bloope had shaken the foundation. And so had Noah. Even innocent little Jason had done his share. It served her right—feeling on top of the world like that. She kicked viciously at a pebble. It was a cockeyed plan from the beginning. Well, all right, so it had worked for Noah. For him it had worked even better than he had planned. He had gotten his little boy and he had gotten Maggie. He would keep one and throw the other by the wayside. Her thoughts were confused.

Had he gotten her? And what did that mean, anyway? Could he throw her by the wayside and whatever was a wayside? What was going on here?

As she walked the sun went down and the sky grew dark. The streets became clogged with traffic and pedestrians, and then they emptied. Still Maggie walked. She paid no heed to the blisters that were forming on her feet from the high heels she wore, nor to the blustery Minneapolis April wind that stung her cheeks.

It was as if he had cut her open, taken out her heart, and squeezed it dry. All her hopes dashed! But why was she blaming Noah? Wasn't it fate she should

180

be cursing? How could Noah suspect that the agency would, out of the blue, change its policy about giving more than one child to each adoptive family? Had he known, he would have applied to different agencies. But he should have known! she thought. He was the one who pretended to be so savvy and wise to the ways of the world. He was the one, after all, who had handled most of the details. But why had she let him? She warred with herself. She should have taken responsibility herself, should have foreseen something going wrong.

On the other hand, what did it all matter? It didn't matter a whit who bore the blame. She was going to be babyless, husbandless, and simply less. She was going to be less happy, less busy, less complete. She was going to be a lesser person. It had all been pie-in-the-sky dreaming, after all. How quickly it had all come down around her head!

And sweet little Jason! Tears formed in her eyes and spilled over onto her cheeks. The wind blew them away, leaving a line of raw skin. The sooner she left the house and that darling little baby, the better. Perhaps Noah would let her visit from time to time. She had visions of herself, years hence, nose pressed against the barbed wire of a schoolyard gate, waiting to catch a glimpse of him. She knew she was being melodramatic, but she couldn't stop herself.

Suddenly Noah's face, contorted from the morning's passion, flashed before Maggie's eyes. Despite herself, she felt a thrill run through her as she relived the magical moments. She shook her head and quickened her step. Nothing made sense anymore. How confused she was!

Suddenly looking around her, Maggie noted that the neighborhood was unfamiliar. It was no longer commercial, nor was it residential. The buildings were old, some appeared abandoned, and others appeared to be warehouses. They were not warehouses like the one that housed her loft, however. These were seedier. A dog howled in the distance. Maggie pulled her spring coat tighter around her. She moved farther away from the alleyways that dotted the area and closer to the curb.

Perhaps she should spend the night in her loft. It had been a long time since she had slept there. She didn't know how she could go back to Brooklyn Park now. Her life there seemed to her nothing but a shadow.

Maggie lay in her bed, looking at the cracks in her walls. In all the time she'd lived in the loft, she had never really noticed how dilapidated it was. Its charm and the sense of independence it seemed to offer her once had blinded her to the cracks. From afar she heard a thumping of footsteps.

She shut off the light and thought of Jason and Noah at home. At home. No, this loft was her home again. She cried despite herself.

The footsteps were getting louder. No one should be climbing, much less racing, up the steps at this hour. "Maggie, let me in. I know you're in there. Let me in right now."

Her heart was an amalgam of fear, uncertainty, and relief. What to do? As the knocking became more insistent she realized that she didn't have much of a choice. She pulled on her skirt over the slip she had been wearing and opened the door to a worried-looking Noah.

"Where have you been? Mrs. Bloope called and told me about the problem and about how upset you were. I called the paper. I called your clients. I even called your mother. I've been sick with worry."

"What do you have to worry about? You've got everything you wanted."

Noah stood in front of her. He stepped toward her to brush a tear from her eye. "Not everything. I want you."

He was being kind and generous. This was a side to Noah she had rarely seen before. But she didn't want his pity or his generosity. The only person she would allow to feel sorry for her was herself. Self-pity, brought on all the more by his charitable posture, lapped at her insides. "You don't have to say that."

"I know." His voice was gentle.

"Then don't." Her own voice was brittle and unyielding. "I accept defeat. You win some, you lose some."

His tone changed to one of exasperation. "What are you talking about? This isn't some kind of game. We're neither all winner nor all loser."

"Pretty words, Noah, but they won't wash." She turned away from him. "You got what you wanted. Now get out of my life and let me be."

She winced at the viselike grip with which he grabbed her arm. "You dope!"

Shaking off his arm, she walked to one end of the large loft and then to the other. She felt used and abused. Seized by despair and panic, she felt like punching her fist through the wall. She was stopped by the knowledge that she would only wind up with a broken fist. "I see you're the type of man, if you were a hunter, who wouldn't believe in merciful killing. You'd want to see your prey writhe and scream before the final death throes."

Noah laughed loudly. "You've such a way with words, dear Maggie. Sarah Bernhardt reincarnated."

She spoke steadily, trying to quell the telltale wobble in her voice. "How can you make fun of me at a

183

time like this? What kind of a person are you, anyway?"

The laughter died on his lips. "I'm beginning to think a person far too good for you."

Maggie stopped short. She passed a hand over her eyes. "Just go, please."

Noah looked uncertain. "All right. But before I do, I'm going to tell you something."

"Oh, really?"

"Really." He took a deep breath. "If you'd stop being so damn self-centered, maybe you'd realize that there are other people who have feelings too."

She strangled the cry that threatened to rise in her. Instead she uttered a shallow laugh. "Let's end this now, oh, you of the deep feelings. Look, I know that you'd like to see me with a baby too. But it didn't turn out that way. I'm not blaming you. The bargain was that you get the first one. Jason is yours. I'm not going to try to take him away from you. Don't worry. I just want to cut my losses."

He stiffened. "Is that what you think? That I came here because I was afraid you were going to try to get Jason? Oh, boy!" He raked his hand through his hair. "You're worse off than I thought. I gave you credit for a lot more intelligence and sensitivity than that. Why, I even thought you were the best thing to have walked into my life. I even changed my attitudes about marriage, real marriage, thinking I'd give it a shot. Maybe I ought to get my IQ tested. Could be I'm suffering from brain damage. You know, from banging my head against a brick wall."

"You're clever, Noah, too clever for me." Suddenly Maggie was devoid of all energy. She didn't even hear his words. She felt weak and exhausted, as if she had been running for hours. She leaned against the back of her sofa. "I'll clear some of my things out tomorrow. A mover will get the rest as soon as possible."

Nervous shadows from a truck's headlights in the street below played on the walls of the dimly lit loft. Noah retreated into the darkest corner near the door so that his face was hidden from view. His voice sounded hollow. "If that's the way you want it." He exhaled loudly. "I'm sorry it had to end like this."

The click of the door as he closed it behind him resounded in her ears like a gunshot. Flinging herself across her bed, she stared fixedly at the ceiling, seeing nothing, feeling only her despair well up inside her like a helium balloon and carry her away. If only she'd been prepared . . . If only she hadn't gotten used to things . . . With the distant clanging of the outside door and the departure of the unwelcome intruder, loneliness claimed her. She couldn't stop herself from weeping.

Then all of a sudden she was jerking her own door open, running barefoot down the cold metal warehouse steps, shouting his name. The echo of her voice bounced off the brick walls and back at her. There was no answer.

Though with no shoes or coat and not dressed for the brisk weather, she yanked on the heavy steel door and ran out into the night. "Noah!" Silence. She looked to the right of her. The sidewalk was dark and deserted save for a black, furry animal that scampered for shelter under one of the trucks that lined the curb. When she looked to the left, she saw a large, bulky-looking figure just disappearing around the corner.

Heedless of the rough pavement, she ran down the long block. As she ran her breathing sounded in her ears like a car's engine. "Noah!"

"Maggie! Is that you?" He came from around the

corner, and when he spotted her hurtling toward him, he moved swiftly to meet her. With arms open wide he caught her and held her and whispered her name.

Her cheek pressed against the softness of his leather jacket, she closed her eyes against the night.

"Maggie, my love."

Lifting her face, she pleaded, "Will you come back upstairs with me?"

She didn't have to hear his answer, for she knew he would come.

"I'm not going to let you walk back barefoot," he said sternly, scooping her up in his arms and striding with her along the windswept street.

She smiled as she put her arms around his neck and lay her head on his shoulder. "This is like a scene out of *Wuthering Heights,*" she whispered.

"Shh, don't spoil it." He carried her easily, as if she were no heavier than a feather. Kicking open the front door of the warehouse, he fairly sprinted up the stairs. With his shoulder he pushed on the door to her loft. It was then, standing in the middle of the great room, that he hesitated. She knew that he was uncertain about where to deposit her. Rightly she guessed that he wanted to lay her atop the bed and join her there. And rightly she guessed that he didn't know whether he should. He didn't know whether it would seal their relationship or doom it.

She rescued him from his quandary. "I guess I'd better wash my feet."

He laughed relievedly. "What I always liked about you was your sense of romance."

From her perch on the edge of the bathtub she told him to make himself at home. "The tap water is nice and cold if you're thirsty. Noah!" Alarm rang out in her voice. "Who is watching Jason?"

186

"Your mother."

"My mother?"

"After my conversation with Mrs. Bloope I called your mother. She came right over."

"She did?"

"Yep. She's a terrific lady. She and Jason took to each other immediately. She's nuts about him already. And Maggie . . ."

"Yes?"

"I'm nuts about you."

She padded over to him, this time with clean feet. "Are you really?"

"Of course, I am."

"You're not just saying that because you feel sorry for me?"

He smiled down at her. "Maggie, I love you."

"Oh, Noah." She felt choked with emotion. "I love you too. I've loved you for a long time. And you know those things I said about you? Well, I didn't mean them."

"I know you didn't." He gestured toward the big windows looking out on the street. "Even if those windows were clean and totally transparent, they would be less so than you. And you know something else? I've loved you for a long time too. I think I knew it was hopeless from the first time I saw you. I think that might have had something to do with my having approached you about the adoption. Maggie," he said as he put his arms around her and moved with her toward the bed, "about that other baby . . . the little girl . . ."

"Hmm?" Her voice and mood were dreamy.

"Well, you see"—he stifled a chuckle—"many thousands of years ago in the Mesopotamian Crescent it was discovered that there's an alternate way to get babies. And I kind of thought that you and I could learn a lesson from those guys back then and start making one ourselves."

Maggie laughed and planted a deep kiss on his lips. "Okay. I think Jason would like a little brother or sister." She pulled him onto her bed and began to unbuckle his belt.

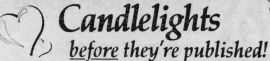

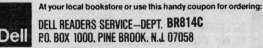